T0161354

PIRATE TALK *or* MERMALADE

Also by Terese Svoboda

Weapons Grade
Trailer Girl and Other Stories
Black Glasses Like Clark Kent
Tin God
Treason
A Drink Called Paradise
Cannibal
Mere Mortals
Laughing Africa
All Aberration
Cleaned the Crocodile's Teeth: Nuer Song

Pirate Talk or Mermalade

Terese Svoboda

DZANC
BOOKS

DZANC
BOOKS

1334 Woodbourne Street
Westland, MI 48186
www.dzancbooks.org

Chapter 1 published at HTML Giant
Chapter 2 published in *Web Conjunctions*
Chapter 4 published in *Fairytale Review*

Published 2010 by Dzanc Books
Jacket design by Brian McMullen
Interior layout by Steven Seighman

06 07 08 09 10 11 5 4 3 2
First edition September 2010
ISBN-13: 978-0982631805

Printed in the United States of America

Heare the mermaides singing

—John Donne

...her body as big as one of us; her skin very white; and long haire hanging down behinde, of colour blacke; in her going down they saw her tayle, which was like the tayle of a Porposse, and speckled like a Macrell.

—Henry Hudson, skirting the polar ice, June 15, 1608

For Bill Raymond and Linda Hartinian

I

1718 - Nantucket Beach

1

I've seen boats as big as this whale. I've seen gryphons the same size, with teeth growing in even as they were taking their last breath.

You have not. And not a live one.

I've been to sea, I've seen all you're supposed to, being at sea. I am sixteen, after all.

If you'd stayed at home, you would've seen to Ma. I'd be a pirate twice, with two voyages under me, if I didn't have that.

Quit your carping. Go stand on its middle. Maybe it will release its wind if you jump on it.

For sure it will stink to heaven if I jump on it.

Let's poke out its eye.

It's a wonder you're not tired of poking whales, a'roving on the ocean like you do, with all the new sail.

Here's the stick—let's do the eye.

Cap'n Peters says there's luck in a whale's eye. Some men use saws on such as the eye, to examine the socket and take away the skull too.

You told this Cap'n Peters about this whale?

Cap'n Peters can see it himself. He's anchored out beyond the neck, nearly done scouring the fresh-wrecked Abingdon. He'll come.

Our greasy luck! Then the sooner it dies the better, and not for anyone but us to collect it.

It's alive all right. Look at the eye.

Help me with the stick. A donkey could haul it out, where could we get a donkey?

If we had a donkey I wouldn't be walking the beach looking for rope to catch the mussels on, would I? If we had a donkey, you wouldn't be shipping out every time the wind blew and leaving me here with Ma, myself only in short pants still and no cutlass.

We need a donkey. The smell alone will bring Peters.

Do you believe in whales? I mean, that they talk?

Two fiddles can talk. One calls, the other says Yes and then some.

Whales dance when there's boats coming with harpoon.

The way pirates do on the gallows.

Not all of them.

They're crying whales, not singing. Poke here.

They swallow the pennywhistle and dance on the tips of their tails on top of the water. And sing.

Whales cry about their future like all creatures worth killing. There's a tear now, with Peters coming. Look—I can make it dance without singing.

Let it be, it's starting to bleed.

I'll let it be with a cut of the knife. If only I had a good one, if only Ma hadn't sold that bit of a blade while I was gone.

She's sold all her brooches, down to the tin-and-garnets.

She sold the true baubles after you were born—or gave them up, cleaned out by whoever she had after you had a father, cleaned out clean as a pike in a trough.

They use beetles to clean the skulls when they're empty. Cap'n Peters says so.

Peters, Cap'n Peters—would he be the one seeing Ma now?

He's seen all of her, if that's your actual meaning. How huge those skull-cleaning beetles must be, so big they can't walk after all that eating, beetles that could eat all of every one of the colonies.

Slippery here, whoa.

Cap'n Peters has got his glass on us now. There, over the wave.

No.

Tease me like you don't know he's watching. Play foot-in-the-water. He'll think we are but careless boys and won't beat us when he sees us.

We are but boys. If I only had a knife—

If you grouse and slaughter the whale before him and he balks and whines, Ma will tie herself to the rafters and I will have to cut her down. It's a poor revenge for her living from one man to the next, though she swears Cap'n Peters is her utter last.

I told you to get her set right, to take Ma to someone while I was off at sea, a woman with a cure.

She wouldn't go, she said she'd have no business with someone like that, she didn't need no one other than Father. She talks to Father from the rafters where you can see the sea out the little window, she talks to you out that window too.

She doesn't know who Father is.

This be true, but still she talks.

This fish is leaking like a ship come ashore.

Whale, it's a whale, not a fish. And if you would quit your poking at the eye, it wouldn't leak so much. Poking it like that makes the sound it makes worse.

You talk like a sea captain with your "Don't this" and "Fish that," a bloody captain, the kind I don't take to.

It's the life of the sea, you said. Yo, HO, HO, you said.

I will give you another punch to match the first.

It breathes—hear it? Cap'n Peters says they are cousin to us.

I can't hear anything while you blather on about Cap'n Peters.

I say we leave it alone because Cap'n Peters will pay us to chop it up. They're bound to want the steaks and oil even if it be old, and some of the bone to hang their hats on, and bone for those who truss up the women.

That's real work, all that chopping.

Aye.

The bone is all I want—I can carve "The Apostle on the Desert" into the bone.

I can carve that—one cut meeting another.

You are a stupid boy. Look—it thinks it is a creature of the land now, it wriggles so. It wants to walk about on its tail.

With the next big wave, let's push it in with our backs.

Let's kill it.

Die, die.

What're you whispering?

Nothing. Die, die, or they'll get you, you whale of us all, you fool whale.

You are whispering.

I'll whisper if I want to.

The whale's dead anyway. Why else would it be on the beach?

Not breathing like this it isn't dead. Not yet.

Look, Peters is bringing his hooks and axes. And a cutlass! There's a knife.

It's soapy-feeling on the outside.

Pitchforks and pries. Let's poke it through to the brain before they get here, let's poke it to make it dead before they poke it, so we can claim it and get the bone. I am grown, after all.

Die, die.

Why do you cry like a girl?

I'm not a girl.

Whale-lover, then. Crybaby.

Listen to it breathe.

I can't hear anything but Cap'n Peters and his men beaching loud like six blacks banging dishpans.

It's breathing big.

There—I've got the stick through, no thanks to you.

It still breathes.

If I hang on it here and pull down, the whole side will rip and they'll know it's ours. Give me a hand—

Home, an hour later

2

Ma, there's rope in my soup

Eat it or you can't watch the hanging.

I can't, not a drop more, Ma. All the chewing hurts my teeth.

It's bone, that's all. Bone against bone. Chew it up, then spit it into your hand. See—a pig clavicle or a horse bone, not rope. Sit still and stop your wheezing and sneezing and snot-dribbling.

The drumming's so loud today, my head hurts.

Old Hubble is getting his practice, best at the dirge in all the colonies I'd say.

There—at the bottom of my bowl—see?

It's a bit of chew. If we sit just right, maybe we'll see the beardtips flame again. I do love the rope.

Ma.

Any less punishment and the ocean would be crowded with rogues.

Put up a rag to curtain it. Father must've been a pirate, I hate these hangings with such a fever.

Eat your soup. And the bones too. I sold yesterday's rope for those bones. And wipe your nose on my skirt. Your father, a pirate—what will you be thinking next? I'm on the lookout for a better man than that, boy, even Peters only takes boats that broke.

Makes a person want to go to sea, your soup.

You'd be your brother then, and curses to you. Hark—here's the catch 'o the day, the pirates walking.

Brother is not so much at sea now.

Brother had better be, and making coin for us too. Such black hair on that pirate—sure to use indigo as anything, in disguise.

Ma.

Stop your sneezing. Were you out standing in the sea this morning? Stay out of the water, you're supposed to pull up the ropes, not go in after them.

The ropes were caught.

Water will kill you, one way or another. Is that the priest waving now?

I could tell but for fat Morgan Little.

He's got to both say the condemnation and the Praise Lord. The magistrate broke his leg this morning climbing a stile and no one else will do it.

Let me go off, Ma.

You don't want that food, it's rotten, only good for throwing. Sit down and eat your soup.

But Ma.

Hush, they're singing now—the pirates are singing. I heard these were merry folk, that they boarded ships singing songs with their knives out full and not between their teeth. That was their mistake, not having their hands free to grip the boat.

They wanted a good cutlass.

Singing makes you brave. Hear how many verses they have? The baker hiding in his hood can't stand still for all this singing.

The baker will dance with his bread.

Look, he's using an old rope today, Master Mason's, the one he dipped his sheep with and can't get out the smell.

You know all the ropes.

I have taught you well enough. Not so much the writing of letters or the sum gathering, but all of ropes and their histories.

Plenty of rope here.

They've soaked his beard in gum. You can hardly see the faces for the smoke.

I wonder how many more are not caught, like mice in hay.

The baker's banged the heads together, jigging them up so close.

I feel it.

The mortal dance ought not to be done without someone watching. Look, look, I say. Fierce they are, and fierce be their Nancies. A sour look or two at choking.

They dance in my soup.

We ought to sell seats here. People like to sit and watch.

People like to press close and not sit, they like to hear everything clear.

It's a shame, having to cut the bit that holds them up,

with the price of rope as it is. But there's a nice length left and I'm sure to get it.

You can never catch your breath after. It's a kind of pleasure for you.

Hold your tongue. I see your friend is picking pockets again, collecting the coppers while they watch it to the end. He'll take his turn.

The far pirate's still shaking.

Where's his family to pull on his leg and break his neck? The baker's cut his rope too soon.

I told you they all don't hang. He must've swallowed a pipe.

Or sung the right song. People do stop their gossip for a miracle.

It's worth living to see a miracle, isn't it, Ma?

Miracles only bring trouble. I've had my own, and worse. Be off with your friend now, and look into the pockets of those who are gaping the most. And don't forget the Cap'n's kit. He'll have something in it for me, if he's not drunk it away already.

All he's come in with is a wreck, and a whale washed up.

Then he's blessed enough and won't hit me so hard. Be off with you.

Don't leave that bench, Ma. I don't want you getting low while I'm gone, and trying the rope.

You're not to worry. All the rope I had was in the soup, knowing I'd get fresh.

3

Go ahead, finish it. Your brother's caught the death of a cold anyhow and didn't take but two spoons of it, only a drink from the bitters.

A real sailor in him, like me, with a taste for bitters.

Real bitters.

The soup's a pip, Ma. You've been stewing the heel of a boot at least, if it's not the cursed albacore straight from the shell.

Eat the soup and tell me what you are doing ashore and not hauling the fish or the fur. Your boat's not due to port for another three months and what coin will I use if you don't sail in with it?

I need a woman for cooking and boiling and such and I've come ashore to marry her, Ma. I will marry a woman who will keep you from making over such soups as this.

The sea has made you bold. But a wife will be another mouth to feed before others in bottom rags come crying with their mouths stretched wide like the robin birds. Only fools marry sailors.

You've married them yourself, I believe.

Marrying a man of the sea is like marrying a boat. They never come home. Or they take to pirating and they had better not.

No pirating for me. I'm set to learn to whittle the whalebone. There's plenty of money in it—I hope to do "The Shepherd's Lad Standing against the Wolf" and "Samson Pulling down the Temple."

Aye, there are many who like it, especially those who are not the seafaring kind, who think sailors go out to look after a pool of fish with birds' feathers and lures and bobbers and spend so little time troubling them that they learn to carve the bone.

Brother can mind the shop, fetch me the customers and light the lamp.

He isn't a boy to mind even his mother, always running about and complaining to me about myself. But how shall we eat while you are whittling thus? Have you drawn a purse from a dead woman's girdle?

I've gained the means. I'll tell you—

Shshsh—not so loud on your luck. Someone comes along the passage now, your brother, I hope, and no one else, with whatever Cap'n has hauled in for me.

To judge from the sound of his dragging, that kit of Cap'n Peters' is ever bit as big as he is.

So I do hope. That's a sneeze! Like a dry drunk with the snuff, that boy.

You'll be killing him with his cold, having to haul such heaviness.

Is that what they say to sailors in a good blow? Is that what they said to my Jimmy?

Father is Jimmy now, is he? The one who died of a sailor's pleurisy? Does this Cap'n Peters prefer to hear of Jimmy over all the others, the snot-drowned sailor of the seven seas?

Where'd you hear of my Cap'n Peters—a'sailing?

It was on land I heard.

Ah, Peters is a brisk fellow, keeps a fine reputation on the docks. Why, many a boat would have him if he weren't about in his own, many a farthing is wagered that he can outsail even the cutthroated pirate. He knows when a boat's going down before she knows it herself, especially out by the neck.

Brother! You've eaten my lot.

She said to.

She would eat it herself anyway during my labors. Which is why you sent me out just then, isn't it, Ma?

This bit of a heel and rope is not worth calling me a glutton, a thief, and a tyrant. A Caligula he thinks me, and that I'll poison myself and him together.

After these many months gone, at least she's the same in her bludgeoning talk. No more height on you, then?

Not unless I stand on a whale.

Ha—you've got your wits about you at least. Ma, take his bowl and fill it with the last boilings—I know you have it somewhere for yourself.

I keep a pot of seaweed worth nothing.

That's the one.

See what the window looks onto now? Where we used to play? The rain tries to hide it.

There's a lot of sawed wood in that.

It's mostly them cleaning the holds of the Spaniards

and pirates—two today. We're always hearing the Dies Irae.

Speaking of the Christian teachings, your brother's come to have the banns said.

You made no mention—

He proclaims it, the sailor who's out of a sail, a man made of romance even grander than yours of pirates. But the fair and first question is—did sweet Cap'n Peters ask after me? I'm the light of his light, what he turns his boat to first after tidying up the beach.

Not so much when I saw him. He has a woman in tow that he claims is his daughter.

Daughter? I'll daughter him. That scum of the ocean—he never talked of a daughter. Did he have her on the breech? Did she come up out of the sea?

Don't grip him like that, his shirt will rip and then where will you get the thread for it?

Daughter, ha.

Ma, don't beat the bearer of news you must already guess.

Your brother cuts me down from my fate to tell me I'm crazy—and then tells me my true love has got up a daughter by way of a voyage.

Open the kit and see what he's brought you.

He's sure to have rope. And there it is. Lovely. From a shop.

I'll soon be setting up my own shop with the bone Peters has promised from that whale.

You chose the bone instead of a share of the oil?

What oil? What bone?

If you weren't always busy in the rafters with your noose-making, you'd hear the news. I found the beached whale that Cap'n Peters is hauling in.

We found it.

You did not tell your Ma.

He checked the ropes while I met the daughter and made Cap'n Peters promise me the bone, just what I need to start my life on land. Peters has towed the whale to a safe place.

It won't be there long.

Keep your tongue in your head. He's a dry captain and doesn't touch a drop.

You need a roof to keep you dry from his drops.

The gibbet for you!

If that's the story, then I'll face Cap'n Peters myself over a glass and pull the bone out of him. I must have the bone to woo myself a wife.

He has this new daughter.

Then the bone be the dowry.

Peters never told you where that safe bone place is, is what I'm a-fearing.

Cut out your tongue and swallow it.

Why isn't he telling me about this daughter to my face? I will string myself up and make a face for him to remember.

I'll take that rope. I might have to tie Cap'n Peters and his daughter to their chairs whilst I go about in removing what is rightfully mine.

Snatching it out of my very hand! It was Cap'n Peters'

gift. Here, take this bit instead that I've been using for the thatching.

The very whelp of the house? The blimey Blessed Virgin Mary I'll take it. I'll take my Ma's hullo, as sour as that, as take the thatch rope, I'll take my leave.

He's better off gone.

He's in a hurry.

I tell you, it's the Harold in him that wants the shore instead of the sea, that medaled officer who wanted a woman on land more than a woman aboard.

The one who built the gallows and then left for England on the press yard fees he stole? That Harold?

Aye, the steps and the string, the same. He was just collecting from Spain by way of England. Died of the gout before he could return, or so the letter that came said.

He left out the best of the gallows' supports, it seems. It leans like the gout itself.

You know as well as I do what makes it lean—too much in the way of business. It was lucky that pirate got away or it would have fallen on the baker from overuse. Now sleep off this chill you're feigning. I will turn over a piece of coal to rid the room of the cold your brother brought from his seven seas.

The bench of sleep.

The gibbetty bench of sleep and the love of a sailor-brother and the sound of the waves and all that land somewhere else that they slap.

He's back for good?

For the good of a woman, not for us.

I'm going to sea with him, Ma. When he sets sail again as he will, because all sailors sail once they do.

You say that and I'll put the poker down your throat, I'll hang myself and drown in a dropper of water. You go to sea with your brother and I will—

Then I will have no reason to return.

You will always be returning. That is the way of those born beside water, of all the water in you from your father, the Captain Edward of the great ship *Whizzen*. One lump or two of this coal that I've stolen out of the bishop's own braziers?

Two, Ma, my true Ma.

Three Months Later

4

I have examined all the varieties of jack-in-the-pulpit in the field, every one, and there are three, I believe, and none of them full-blooming which makes the naming of this variety that much more trying. I also bring a specimen of penny frog for you that I have caught here in the folds.

Girls don't take off their bonnets to catch frogs in them. Not even girls using a cane.

You do if you are teaching Winthrop, the half-wit heir. Peters knows the game and has instructed me well. Have you seen the boy?

My brother says you can have too many frogs in a field. He said they push up Dead Man's Fingers for one thing and I told him—

Alive, alive-o.

This one is squashed about the foot. What can I learn from that, that you, with your lameness, cannot teach?

It is a frog from the inside that is most worthy of examination, very like a person perhaps.

Dead Man's Fingers are not so much a part of a person, are they?

A plant like the mushroom, their companions. Many of those fingers grow in the marsh behind, the one that is home to all these frogs.

Catch the frog, kiss the frog and like it.

I'm not going to play your silly game. These are lessons for the boy really—where is he?—and you'd best not be about at all.

Teacher, teacher. I can tie a Hugenot, I can lift a bull.

A bull-calf. I am sixteen too, you know. Almost old for a teacher.

I am your elder by a week and not ugly to you, Miss Count-Your-Pupils. The fiddler last night played only for your feet I suppose.

I made my way. But you cannot even sign your name to paper.

I am familiar with every family of seabird and all mathematics up to geometry, so long as I don't have to write the sums out.

That is what you claim.

And you? How about the sum-making you puzzle over in your teaching, your froggy subtractions?

I have added all the varieties and those that I counted four paces from the tree bearing a name from Linnaeus that the boy studies. Of them all, the sum is 258, in other words, taking the three plantings of snowberries minus 136 makes 122 posies, added and subtracted both. But where, I am now asking, are all those posies now to make up such a sum? What's become of them?

Here you are.

Oh, no! Oh, no! These are supposed to provide lessons in adding and subtracting for all of the next week. Now I will have to go back to the book, I will have to teach the boy from the book. Oh, why did I ever leave the sea?

Don't screech so. If the boy's father hears—

Oh dear, oh dear.

Please don't sob. Crying won't obtain for you a way out of teaching. I will though.

Bother! You will fill me up with children before I'm grown. I am the first of my family to become a teacher, a family in which no one has ever read before, or even pretended to.

Cannot Cap'n Peters read?

He is less my family than you know.

Some say that, though the taking of orphans as salvage is common enough.

It is nothing shameful. I was combing my hair on a rock.

And Peters?

He treats me most cruelly.

It is the way of men.

Not all men. I saw your brother weeping at the whale.

You did not.

I am your teacher and your better, I know what I've seen. And I know where the bone of the whale is, those bloody bones.

Of course you do.

Don't stand so close. My cane!

I wish to trap the small insect you described as comely where it has landed on your shoulder.

Oh—of the genus which includes the beetle of which there are thousands? But this is the only one with seven or nine marks on its wing.

Nine marks. I make good progress but you will not bless the work.

Please—there should be more than ample room on this escarpment for both of us.

Room for twenty more dry-eyed angels such as yourself?

You must practice the writing of your name. I have showed you the E. You must form it in the air every day, and on the ground if you are lacking paper.

A noble letter, E.

If you can't write your name, you will be beholding to many.

Beholding to you, perhaps? In reading, the letters bend and float away and will not stay.

Reading is like a sea voyage, you either attend to it and see the world, or you stay at home. *Tristram Shandy* was tossed over many a ship, which is how I at last learned the skill.

You know nothing about the sea—you never teach it.

Nothing that is known about the sea is true.

So you say.

I shall teach you just the beginning: How the Sea Was Formed. A carpenter cuts a king's worth of trees and lays them flat to each other, then nails them together with the teeth of all the birds that fly which is why so few birds have teeth now. When he has finished, the wood makes the bridge from this land to the next. Still, it must be painted. The carpenter has blue powders left over from coloring the sky. The strength of this paint to adhere to the air is very great but the power of it to stick to the wood is so much more. What is left puddles before the carpenter can put down rags to stop it. In most places, where the blue collects, it shines darker than the sky but elsewhere it runs into the sky and joins it. Under the strength of this blue, the birds' teeth loosen and fall out and then the teeth sink into the sea, only later to float up to the beaches as shells. The boards themselves, as blue and as lively as they are, come loose and change into the rafts that drift by the drowning who can't find the bridge for all the blue color.

I would not guess it.

Man cannot fly but he can swim.

Some, I have heard. I can't. Water has always crept up and filled my shoes with trouble or taken our roof. Only when it buoys a boat do I want to venture upon it. My Ma screams in fear of it.

Your Ma has been taken too much by it.

Some sailors have had her, even from the far seas, and roughly too. I think it is why she loves the rope so, she dreams of belaying herself to land at last.

If I did not have these curls to keep, I would show you how gently the waves lift and hold your arms.

You will always have curls to mind.

I will.

Dust to dust, as the church says, not water to water.

Water to water.

I get seasick just hearing you say that. The way you sing it.

Water is ever more prevalent than earth. How many days can you journey by sea? How many by land?

I do not journey these days. I am a poor boy who studies but what you tell him.

Let me say then I think it is time for you to immerse yourself. Listen to my song. Come, come—

But your curls—

Over here. Through the rocks. The song.

There are currents. There are terrible fish. The waves—

Take my blasted cane! Waves to hold you, waves to— ah, Winthrop.

Snake! Snake!

Unbanded. I believe it is harmless, but you can't be certain about one so orange along the tail. Hold it tight about the head, or it will bite you. Count the colors as it dies.

It's dead, Winthrop. You're going to die.

Don't put fear into him. He might tell his father and his father will have you jailed for stealing his lessons.

The boy is slow, and will be slower.

Leave the snake in the thicket and go along. That's a fine boy.

A boy with a fine purse.

The water—

I want no more to do with water, I want a berth on shore, with the whale's bones and a woman who can carve its bone where I instruct. It is your own Cap'n Peters whom I fear has drunk the bone down.

Your Ma is ill over Cap'n Peters.

Cap'n Peters is ill over you. I will give you my name, make you a fortunate wife with an honest hearth.

The time is near when a woman will not need to set her hand in contract. Why not give her merely a set of numbers as can be found in any book to suffice for a term of possession, and not the name of a man? There are surely enough numbers, and more.

You are certainly a clever teacher and will make a clever wife.

Cease tempest-crying over that snake bite, boy, and press the burdock against it. Keep your hand over the wound where it swells too, that's right.

You know so much about these things?

You must address me with belief in your voice.

Belief is a learned thing, like writing.

You do not learn your way to me.

Ways open daily like routes between blocks of ice athwart the bow that the brave sailor faces so often before his triumphant return.

Remove your hands from me. I will have the boy's father lash your back to ribbons, with Cap'n Peters providing the whip.

Are these Dead Man's Fingers?

Brother! I told you to stay away and ask questions later.

Point them toward the sky. Pray, point them up to where the blue clouds await their carpenter.

She is full of cant. You talk to her. I'll see you later at Ma's.

What do you two whisper of?

Of how prettily you speak of carpenters and clouds.

Thank you. Your brother is less sure of his words.

He is unused to women, having been at sea. That makes him a bad judge of their wiles. I know women from my Ma.

What about us is wily? I am as open as a hand. As for you, it's not the Dead Man's Fingers you want, it's the full hand of a life you can spend. Here, open your own.

What ho! It's as hard as marble, with the blue of a wave inside.

The whale's eye. It should be dry and gone by now, eaten by cats. I found it in amongst the sycamore leaves, left from when that poor whale was taken asunder. Have it and study it. I like the way you laugh.

My brother is not watching? He will see nothing?

Nothing, I swear it. He cuts his thumb sawing on a stick as if it were bone, and sucks the wound.

5

As tractable as a dog, she was.

A hound, I think. A harrier.

Likening me to dogs! When I think of all the trouble you've been.

Ma, don't talk. You're making bubbles of the blood.

I tried to return you after the theft but the family was gone, in grief I suppose. I was in Hampshire or Maudin's, a'laundressing, or making the swords' scabbards, or looking to the curling goods. I remember the sea and the stink of civet cat. It was after I fell in—and out—with the maharajah.

The leech that was left for her—find it. I think it's crawled beneath the chest.

The man kept civet cats, fifteen of them. For the perfume. Baltrick was the name.

Not Kinnell?

Kinnell once gave me a trinket beaten out of gold. He's the one who urged your return. At Godspeed, he shouted, over your infant cries. It could've been Reverend Baltrick. Or the maharajah.

No water—let her speak. Her lips still move.

The stealing wasn't hard. A loaf under the blanket in

place of you.

Which of us is stolen, Ma?

They wouldn't pay my price to fetch you back. Or they didn't receive my sign. They went sailing after the maharajah.

Peters' route? The high one?

Don't ask her more, she can't speak.

She speaks.

A cow bellows better with a beet stuck in its throat, she struggles so.

What, Ma?

I wanted lads to fetch and cover me on the occasions when I had drunk overmuch, and to carry water that I should not have to do it myself with all my fine husbands.

I'll close her eyes.

Don't touch me.

That was surely the last breath.

Another.

I found a penny here, beneath the sheet.

You will need two.

Not if you never close your eyes, Ma.

I was in Hampshire—or Maudin's. A man came up out of the sea. He had arms only, such arms.

What sailor was this one?

Manuel, a man from the seas of the south. He had a big mustache, and he wept that I should hold him.

A mustache like my brother's?

She has no more to tell.

She is finished now.

She stirs.

He left, and I wept an ocean.

I'll hold her up. Take a breath now. Did she ever tell us true?

She made the soup, she called us sons. You don't waste breath on a deathbed.

But she only clouded the water.

Listen. That was surely the departed rattle, that last. You can't wake the dead.

She's green about the face—

Don't go to sea, I tell you, don't.

The sea? But—I will go, like brother.

We all go. What else?

Ma! Ma! Quiet yourself.

One of us is stolen, if not us both, and one of us—

The mustachioed man, the sea—

Ma!

She is surely done now. Open the window. Here is the mop. I'll lay the coins.

It was just something she said. Look—I have her nose. She is my mother.

And I have the height of the beggar on Bond Street. Who is our father?

Are we even each other's?

We were too young to know if that were true.

At least I will no longer find Ma hung on a rope everywhere.

Use the mop on your tears. What a woman you are.

It was her great wish, to be hung by her own hand. If she'd have just cut the mussels off the rope, she wouldn't have suffered so. The terrible wounds at her neck. The coughing into it. She didn't trust the baker. Those are badly crossed buns, she'd say to the baker and not put a penny his way.

Yes, yes. We'd better be doing the washing ourselves now, or the flies will take Ma to her rest.

Each fly with the face of Ma, each face the same and not ours.

We are men complete now, we need no mother. For a scene in whalebone: "The True Mother Greeting Her Lads."

Surely the true father is dead. So many years have passed and not many live out their time.

There are tales about fathers who die and leave their estate to those who have been stolen away. It bides us well to consider this.

Not if he crawled out of the sea.

Or died of the snot, like Jimmy. Or built the gallows.

Or stole the bones of a whale with drink.

Or a dozen others.

A new woman we need more than a father. A woman to cook and carry the water.

Aye, water is the point of all this.

6

It's too cold to even drag a nib over paper, let alone write my name.

You'll be writing on a block of ice in midwinter to learn the signing, that's what she said. And here we are.

Why must I sign a marriage contract? It's just a delay, one of so many.

It can't be so difficult if she can.

It's easy for her. Her name is shorter by so many letters.

Until she gets ours. She says I remind her of her sister.

What—you?

Some way I make my laugh.

After I make my mark, you won't need to laugh with her again. Oh, but what if someone sees how I sign and uses that for himself? I'll make my money without all this writing, and as for marrying, she can sign for us both. Besides, I'm sure to topple the bottle just keeping the paper in order.

My sister Kate, she said, would advance the argument thus: If he can't write his name, he can't give it to you.

Peters is all the family she has. Oh, bother. So few of the seabirds yield the right nib for a seaman's hand.

You should have swum when she asked.

Am I a donkey to be tested to see if it is worth the sale?

You don't swim either, no one swims in the sea if they can help it. I wouldn't swim even for the bone.

Or a wife?

I need to spread my name with offspring, not with a nib.

I don't understand why she doesn't put the test to someone else.

I am a man of high quality.

Just learn your name and write it or I will.

Threats, idle threats. I suppose the devil needs a signature too.

Put the curve there. I bought you a bit of tallow so you can see the paper after the sun sets.

The sea takes an X. You can join a crew with just a mark. Why couldn't Peters have taken up with someone less taxing?

She's slapping herself in the next room to keep the cold off, she's tapping her cane.

Waiting's a good lesson for someone whose relation could drink up a whole whale's bone, as he may well have. Not to mention my own waiting, my soul dragged out and around for these many months, trying to find out what she wants.

It's not Peters she wants. His signing is wrong

You have spoken to her in confidence?

We were waiting for you to bring the paper.

Ach—I'll teach the teacher—about waiting. We will wait in the cold, and not write.

I must've slept.

You snored to heaven.

What now? The ink has frozen in a puddle.

But you managed it—look.

I did that? I don't remember— Is the fire out? Let me sleep just a little longer.

I'll take it to her.

The tails be a little long.

The way my sister would make it, if she were one of us. Your finger is stained.

I dropped the ink.

It is your hand on this paper.

No, no. –Aye. I did it to reduce the steepness of my distress, having to listen to him all these months. Now the banns can be said and it can be over.

You are female. I see it now.

What? I am my mother's son.

There is more mystery under the roofs of bakers than inside your smalls. Let us all meet at Eben's Kettle.

Peters would hide the bone here, with the very weft of the sea underfoot, a smuggler's hatch in the floorboard to load unseen from the water.

It's not in these rooms, neither of them, that I can discover.

Are you wanting me for the bone or for myself?

For your cleverness, for then others will know your teaching as my own wife's, for your shapely hands, for your gentle way with a needle—

At least you learned the courting well enough. Take the bone as my vengeance to Peters.

There's bone sticking out above the tideline—where the snow starts.

We'll return grateful, my dear. Then the banns.

That's a strange bit of singing she's making.

It's the wind. The wind howls and chills her.

Do you believe she's a'witching, brother?

She's a woman, brother.

Aye, she's that. And found combing her hair at the sea.

She combs her hair at all hours and places. I'm taking her to the parson to be married—not like Ma and her doings—and then I'll build a house away from the sea, with the door facing the land.

She won't like that.

It'll be a relief to her. Is that Peters? Go to the turn in the road to see.

I'll pile the bone into the sack.

She's gone.

You were sent to check the road—she's gone?

I looked behind the door and around and under it all and into the hatch hole. There's her cane.

She didn't pass by here, I didn't take my eye off the road.

The hatch was laid open, the water swallowing there as angry as ever.

Bother the woman. I don't see her marks anywhere.

She told me stories about a carpenter and his boards, why the horns are doubled on caterpillars, and how two Welshmen found gold in the mountains.

Cap'n Peters will say we drowned her for the bone.

Is she swimming under the ice? She does like the water here, even the icy water.

That's what queered Cap'n Peters to her, her winter swimming.

She could be in the woods, naming the winter buds, getting past us. We will go walking and find her petting an ermine she's found wild.

She was always looking for someone to sign or to swim. Well, the ocean will keep her only for a few days or she'll be found in the ice in the spring. Let's go. We've got the bone.

We can't leave without her—

There are fish in the sea, hungry fish looking for what they can find. If Cap'n Peters catches us, we'll be judged wrong for sure.

No, no, no.

Stop up your eyes. She was my woman, at any cost, cripple or not. She was mine. Who's that—Peters coming through the drift?

It's her, of course.

It's his saws and scythes. Run!

II

7

Mr. Shanks, Mr. Luggams—a fine day for the tropics. Not too buggy. All that sugar loaded on the *Mary Stewart* will attract the bugs.

You bloody well threw yourself at them, you did.

They'll take us on, I know it. I've seen them around with the card players and darters, fetching up crew with a hard knock to the noggin. We'll save them the trouble.

Isn't it enough that we fair escaped Cap'n Peters on the first vessel we found? Peters would've had us lashed to his bow if he'd caught us. To be caught as a pirate is bullocks' worse.

I've seen a pirate get off, go running down the street with the rope still tied around his neck.

Idiot. I must talk to Sitwell. I overheard him say he had positions working with the watches and clocks. I'd be good twisting flax, preparing the strap to bind a watch to the pocket. It's like the cutting of bone, the same careful fingers. Why, I'll soon be buying bone from my wages, carving "The Shepherd Lad Standing against the Wolf" in a trice.

He's sure to have cutlasses, watch man that Sitwell is, sure to have swords in his cupboards as springs and tallow. You're the one who dropped the bone when Peters was upon us.

Two hills past the dock, Sitwell said.

He just needs someone to lift his goods and drive his

horses. A bought slave you'll be to Sitwell.

I say I must try his offer. I am the elder and I know my mind. Anyway, we can't go home with Peters prowling for us.

Here you could be a chimneysweep as well as a watchman, the competition's not so great here as elsewhere, especially with so few chimneys.

No chimneys.

You could sweep, sweep your way up while I'll be eating toad-in-the-hole three times a week on board a boat as black as soot—and you'll be sooted. Instead of buried myself, I'd like to bury a chest full of treasure. It's either the plague or the biting of insects that'll get us here on land, dead as doornails. To the sea I say, to pirating.

I hate the sea life. I worked the docks, I never did sail.

Brother!

Repairing the ropes and hawsers. Rope is in the family—at least Ma's. I had all the tall tales of the life of the sea, without the spray. I did as Ma begged us—I stayed ashore.

So sick you were of the tilt and slosh coming over, I did wonder your sudden loathing.

Aye.

My own brother making up a life he didn't spend.

Aye.

But seeing Shanks and Luggams debouche the dock with all their booty, so brazen with their loads in broad daylight! And how they fill out their snuff with the dust of gold! I think those pirates who get hanged are done for the greater good of the thieving that is done to us, such as the removing butter from the dairyman's cart.

That butter was for Ma. And only once before I went to sea. Or did not.

You've got the pirate blood in you, you just need the place to shed it. In a few strikes of the clock, Luggams and Shanks will put their feet upon the deck again, time enough for us to gather provisions, to buy that new blade you admired yesterday with what little coin we have left.

These two do sail a big ship, with double masts. I don't wonder at your temptation.

Pirates are just sea folk who work for themselves. I think you lack the strength for the pirate's life.

I can lift a bull and anchor. I have the strength—on land.

Beat me in the balls for a fortnight if pirates don't do well with the ladies, that much I do know. They don't cast out nets or drag long line, women come running to them. Not like that last woman you had.

The pirates' women invite their friends around to your execution, set a table with cakes and ale under the gallows, and bring your only child to it.

Ah, but the mermaids don't fear the pirates, and they're thick as shrimp hereabouts.

A mermaid is just a woman not grown, one who snatches at men and leaves the offspring to comb out her hair. Not a pretty enough picture for me.

Shanks and Luggams have repaired to the fo'castle. They won't be there long, the crew's hauling sail.

Go then, you don't need me.

Need has nothing to do with it. It is as a courtesy I'm asking you to come along, landlubber though you be, as your brother I'm asking you. Our trust be doubled and our profits too, onboard as pirate brothers.

We may not be such brothers as you think, if Ma died true.

We must hunt our true father and start our true lives. Our father will not find us, that's for certain. Let's roll the whale's eye for an answer. Left, you pirate, right, you stay.

Where did you come into that eye?

Found it in a drift of sea spindle.

It could be mine, part of the bone I tried to claim.

You'll drive me to the pirate life, with your bone found in every bone.

Well, I know what's good for me without throwing the eye. There's your Luggams now. I'm sure he'll take you onboard like lice to a bird.

Mr. Luggams! Here!

Be off with you. The ocean's too much a cradle for a man so grown as myself.

I'm good on the fo'castle, Mr. Luggams. I've had years of it.

Indian Ocean

8

You don't know the glory of being hung on a hook and dragged by your lip when you must leap from the water just to ease off the pain. Pull it out!

It will leave a gash if I pull it straight.

I keep seaweed at the bottom that defies the wounds of the flesh. How else does a fish last with a grimace of hooks?

You departed so strangely, the winter upon us, and Peters fast approaching.

It had to be.

I have the whale's eye still. Will that help?

Don't show it, there be sailors about even in the dark of this clouded night and the ship's heaving to the gunwhales. It might roll away.

I'm sorry to catch you.

I'm glad to be caught. When I saw it was your hook, I rejoiced. Just wrench out the barb. I will brace myself against you and the rail, tight.

There.

That's better. I have been hauled up by the mouth four times looking for you and your brother, each time promising this and that until they tossed me over.

This fishy part is new and shocking.

Not so new. The skirts all women wear to confound men hid it. The cane laughed at you.

Strange, I don't hear the ocean when I am beside you, the deck does not roll. I've been onboard for over a year now and nothing like this has ever happened.

Night brings its own confusions. I will instruct you on the history of the night sky, as I have your brother about the sea. Four poles cut from saplings are given out at the world's edge next to its furious wind, the one that enjoys whipping such poles when they are still barked and leafed. When the two ends are pushed into the earth, the wind rips so hard at the spaces between the curve they make with the other poles that the skin of the earth comes up at the edge like a rug upturned. This underside glows with the iridescence of underground creatures who have crawled by their own light inside the ground. Now they smolder in the night sky. Not everyone believes their light is made of fire because they're so cold but lay your hand on ice and pull it up fast—it too burns.

All the night talks when you talk, even with such a gash.

Together we will tell Father you have been found.

I know nothing about this father.

Yes, you do.

Stop grabbing at me, stop it. The water is fearsome, the ocean is death. I am alike in this with my brother—we do not enter the water.

That is one truth you will have to pierce for yourself.

I am a pirate now, and know only my own intent.

Best for you to hold fast to the whale's eye then, for luck.

What kind of luck is that—it's drowning you're offering.

I heard Cap'n Peters went under a fortnight after we sailed, swallowed up by a cup of tea, his heart crushed, losing you.

He was in want, after your Ma departed, telling stories about her so even the sea could hear.

Watch your bleeding mouth. Ma did not know his wants after you arrived.

That's what your brother says. Who can know the heart of a woman, especially one like your Ma?

Perhaps it is my brother's heart that is unknown.

Tell him you've seen me treading the waters, go ahead.

I would rush up the mast and shout your name but he's not onboard, he didn't take the oath, not seeing the pirate life for what it is, a port a'glitter at every call, swords a'plenty and no landholder taxing every tomorrow. My brother continues his oath against all water by staying off it.

A sea of tears, perhaps.

His letters are smeared, it's true, but someone else writes them. Quiet, it's Shanks abroad.

A night catch! What a fisherman you are. I see from all the blood you've stuck it well. I'll finish the gutting and offer you the liver if it's of a size. Keep your hand on it while I fetch my good knife.

Over now, quick.

9

Give that back—it is my only shawl, it is the shawl you married me in.

I haven't had a watch to do for months—we can't eat a shawl. We must trade it for bone so I can triple our profits.

Go to the ends of the earth, and sail to where the serpents lie. To sell my shawl for an inch of whalebone—bone that's no good even in a pot!

People pay well for a picture on it—but there won't be much left after I settle the chits you've written clear across the island.

Better than written across my tombstone. How I rue offering you my timepiece for your improvements. For just a look, I said. And you looked and looked.

It was you who took the glass off the works, who pulled the stem.

You said I needed a minute hand, I said there were too many hands already.

Gladness fills me to know those works have stopped. Now I will be cutting this bone, and people will like it. The port is a'swarm with new folk off the boats, and overseers who need to know when to quit the slaves. It's busier here than London, it's the center of the world in commerce—and in fashion too.

You thought people would like a feather stuck on the works to brush off the flies.

There are few who appreciate my timepiece thus far, with or without the flies, but with my improvements—

Only fifty-three here keeping the time or the like, less your own watch which I hide, and the ships' clocks, when they are in port. Even if you wind each of them every week, there are still only fifty-three to divide with Cyrus.

He must be of noble birth to gather the business so quickly, regardless of what he says, a duke at least or a—

He is too handsome by half, yes.

I think you'd be just as pleased to be without a shawl, to show yourself.

Oh, let the ocean take you.

Cyrus, Cyrus—she's yours.

Close that window, you fool. It's market day.

I should be down there beside Cyrus, listening to him unhook the watches out of the waistcoats of the wealthy by his very words. Never has there been so many who needed oil in their works or their clockhands reset until he opened his shop.

And where were you?

You had dresses a'plenty until Cyrus washed up.

You did nothing about him, always mooning over getting the bone or moaning over your brother, the foul pirate. Give me that shawl back.

From where, pray tell, do you get the cotton for your petticoats? Stolen of the pirate. The cocoa for your cups in the morning? The pirate. The lovely Madeira? Even the ribbon in your hair be blue only on account of the pirate's indigo. The foul pirate.

Don't you think Cyrus is a handsome one? He's four years your younger.

Quiet, woman. I'll not have you scull the bottom for daggers. I will take the *Hope* to the last port if you drive me to it, and leave you behind. I will, even though I fear a voyage at sea more than I fear your noise and bother. Keep the shawl.

Cyrus! Cyrus!

I am so easily rid of?

We have no children. You were too timid.

That is your own doing. Or not doing. But this too can change, knowing the temper of your heart and of Cyrus' desire. But not with myself as witness. I will sign ship's papers today, I will.

I believe you will. And let it be a long voyage out—on the *Hope.*

My luck will leave with me.

Perhaps—but what if Cyrus will not have me?

You think so little of me that I must bear such a question? Fruit falls from the trees here, winter cannot harm you. You have your shawl. But I would hoard your petticoats too if I were you. The daughters of others are younger.

And eager, even for a tradesman such as he. You should send for me then, as soon as you come into money.

And blacken my future further?

How will you rise in the morning with a starched collar and leggings without holes? And eat as quickly as you can seat yourself? Answer me.

I now know the compromises a man makes. You are an expensive charwoman who spares me nothing. The years I have spent with you.

Two—no more.

Put that pot down.

I shall not until you receive damage.

Amazon!

10

The sails like a curtain, stars and then no stars.

My mother loved the line, especially the rope as thick as the mate's wrist. Even my brother worked the line, in secret, though on land, not the sea. You'd like my brother, though you'd put fear into him with all your fierce tattoos.

A man must be his own placard if he has lived out a legend. Rain behind that swell of stars. There—through the straights.

A squall?

A squall.

That last lightning nearly stopped my heart.

Those were good flashes.

Luggams says in the worse of storms, the lightning goes green and runs up the rigging.

Hear the singing?

No singing in these straights. Luggams hates the singing.

It can't be the fish, singing.

Luggams forbids all singing whatsoever now that Shanks is gone. He doesn't like the caterwaul of cats neither but cats we have to have, for the vermin.

Aye. The pigs we shipped before would at least dance,

they would eat out of your hand for a sniff of bread.

Pigs will eat your hand.

A pirate bunch, pigs. I wish we had some still.

If you eat at all, best eat in private, with yourself alone on the poop deck, or else someone will fight you for it.

Not for me the poop deck. The stink!

Clean as the Pope's hand. All that is left to eat is shoes, and those who have them have chewed them soft as chamois.

I think Luggams chews on gold coin.

His teeth show it. A doubloon on a starving ship is as good as a shell cast upon a beach.

The second mate's tied a Spanish coin to his line to lure the fish.

Good luck to him! I do miss the turtle's banging.

A great turtle it was, two hundred weight if it were one.

Now there's a beast—it didn't eat for four months and still tasted sweet.

I once had luck fishing in the night. Once only, and didn't eat it, though the fish be bigger than even that turtle.

Why not, by the boils of St. Augustine!

You don't hear the singing?

No songs, none. Boil the sand inside that whale's eye you pocket and eat that.

That's hardly fish. You'd do better to keelhaul yourself and pray you scrape barnacles off the bottom of the boat with your chest. They attend only to god, these fish below.

Minister fish, a whale. The second mate will catch nothing.

Or the fish will catch him, like Shanks, out from the bottom of a wave. That shark leapt like a marlin to catch him. I felt sorrow for the shark, having Shanks to chew. Here, wet this bit of knot and snap it at the watch in the crow's nest. Leeward, now.

Those were real curses. My brother used to say pirates cursed for nothing, just to put fear into anyone's hearing, but I think we curse most often to hear ourselves alive.

More like fiends than men. Let us curse altogether and get the sails up.

Bloody sails. I do miss the Yo, ho, ho. I wish Luggams would have it.

Turn your head thus and sing yourself:

Booty, ho! By the blood of Our Lady.
Booty, ho! Put gold to my shingles
and pied silver to my latch
and teeth all gold in a row—
Booty, ho!

Mind the line there.

I'll bury my gold and live out my days full to the ears with grog and no one will come around accusing me.

To have lost every penny of the last run.

They were bigger than us.

Bigger, ha. Too bad about the booty. You voted for Madagascar?

The Cape, the Cape is the way. Prizes going to the bottom of the ocean for want of pirates at the Cape.

We'll need a heap of wind to get there.

And a bit of bread or a haunch. With a spit turning right on deck, and dandyfunk, and flip in our cups to the top.

Gunpowder punch! Wait, the line be fouled there.

I'll lend you a hand. That last island we tried, there was a lad who swam out— He looked so like yourself. A copy in black.

So they say. 'Tis a favorite island of mine, it is. I've stopped and gone down a dozen times.

Others have called it a little Boston, after you.

Once or twice, I admit, we've had to pull anchor in haste. See the dawn star off port?

Aye.

That's no storm coming before it with the daylight—a sail's upon us.

Ahoy!

Ship ahoy! Arm yourselves!

It's a terrible moment when you thrust your head over the side, a-scrambling for purchase when they could stick your throat so easy—

Aye, and we go ahead in this wind so slowly you'd think we were towing our pots astern and the mattresses.

Huzzah!

A Day Later

11

Ocean makes me sick.

Grog makes you groggy. Land made you landbound. Drink a little saltwater to let the sea settle in. Pirates always take a dose just before the swells start.

I won't fall for drinking one of your wee grogs a second round. There I was, about to land and start a new life—

Of clocks and watches! Not even your beloved bone. I've saved you twice tonight, once from the other cutthroats aboard, and once from your own life.

Did you have to hit me bang on the pate quite so hard?

You'll get used to it.

I'll never be getting used to taking blows from my own brother.

This is a pirate ship.

Yes, yes, so they say. Just make up a paper that declares you took me by force then I'll give you no trouble. You have me now, brother, in the burden of a prisoner.

Hush. You're no prisoner. Luggams remembers you. He's taken you on to pull my mate's line.

Is that so? I am sorry to have killed your mate.

You did not have to run him quite through.

I did! I did have to run him through! He would've done the same to me.

My mate was fair that way, though you would have liked him. From Boston, where the Tattoo King put his marks upon him. Here, take the sail hand-over-hand with the needle and mend these exploded holes. At least the man had sons a-plenty.

And you have regained a brother.

But lost a cutlass.

He fell to the deep at my single thrust.

He did. Throw me the line.

But I thought pirates kept chests full of weapons, everything shared, that's what I thought, and then divided it in the pirate way, which means, for one, I should have seen a bit of what we were hauling that you ate right after the taking? At least a bit of it. When does the cheese from my boat stop at me, with the haunches of lamb, sheep and beef, given out in the proper pirate's way? On a regular vessel at least they offer around the gristle.

Stop, you must stop. Every boat rides its own sea, whatever it becomes. Do you think we sign in a circle, the way they tell it, or swear upon a hatchet instead of the Bible? Smith, the quartermaster, tells it true.

They call him quartermaster, this lawless brine-mouthed bunch?

This be the pirate life, says Smith, the new pirate's: he should be tarred so that his skin turns pale, as pale as a turnip—that is, after all the peeling—and that it is the paleness that kills the cowards and not the sharks he screams to be fed to, all blown up with white after the tar's gone, and bleeding red blood through the skin. Pale as a turnip—it is a nice turn of the tongue. That's the start of a pirate life got right, the way Smith tells it. You wait.

A story like that's why I prefer belowdecks, I'll take belowdecks anytime. Without the sea in my face, I can think of the land.

No air below except a rat's cough. I'm for sleeping under the sheets midships and chancing I'll get my throat cut when someone slips on board to right the wrongs and retake the treasure, such as we did on your boat. A great wont of treasure on your boat I might add, unless we count the watch plaitings.

Treasure for some. You didn't have to throw every bale over.

You won't be wanting those plaitings now anyway, that job is gone. You can get the boat's works set straight for us instead.

Set me off on land!

Here be the Smith I was telling you of.

The two of ye quarrel so, you'd think you were made of one mother, bad luck to us and to you both. They say brothers save each other and none of the rest.

We are not so much brothers, not really. Not according to our Ma. Besides, we quarrel away, and stick the loser.

I fought with the brothers Bungleston who raged the seas the back end of the '80s. Aye, I served under the Roger— not the jolly, mind you—and for fun, one brother would take a plank and magic it right across the water, over one wave and another, and sometimes he would signal to us, all the while sinking into the foam. Fish took the other brother when he, for spite, at last put the board under himself and sank straight down. Brothers they were for sure.

A danger to themselves and others.

But this boy's got arms on him that could lift a barrel of sand and a face that would belay a mother, if she saw two of them together. You boys keep the deck quiet with yourselves if you can, and take the watch whilst I have a hand of whist, and wait.

Aye, aye.

Aye. Aye, aye, aye.

You are giddy, fearing for your life.

I can't stop laughing. What were the chances of my own brother falling prey to us? At least I can laugh, I am falling down laughing at that. It's time to laugh.

We are the only two aboveboard now.

Not so loud. We have a job to do.

We?

Tie the wheel down, brother.

What is about to happen?

Luggams knows. He's folded his spyglass like a snail's trick and taken it below.

Brother?

I'm the pirate captain now, like atop the whale. If you weren't so green, you could scale the ropes and sing out verses from the f'osicle in honor of Luggams who hates them.

You remember wrong about that whale. It were me atop.

You were gouging at the eye, the bloody eye. I stood atop and heard it sing.

It were the woman Peters took, singing.

She couldn't sing, she could only count.

You weren't listening. I wish I had a cutlass. I don't like the quiet.

They do keep a chest full of cutlasses below.

I knew it so.

They sort them after a boat-taking such as yours. Myself, I snatch any one that comes my way. Roger and Ebert, the plunder lads, they'll be joining us at the next ocean.

I'd like one with bone at the hilt or a ruby and a broad blade like an Indian's.

Leave the whalebone and watches and you might make a pirate yet.

A cutlass, just for protection. To cut my way back to land.

Hear that?

You could hear a bream breathing. That's nothing.

You don't know the half of the fear that swims under to get at you. All seamen worth their salt—and that's heaps of salt—know there's strangeness under their feet, about how it's us or our cousins at the very bottom, walking around as usual, breathing in and out the actual water.

It's a strange life, the sea life, I'll grant you that.

Soon you'll have the look of the strange yourself.

All this glug-glug-glug of grog, and the hold, and me with a bump on my head.

One of the others would've quartered you with two blows.

This be the price I pay, this and the yo-ho-ho. I hate the water more than before. Hear it again?

That's weather, that's nothing.

A hole's starting in the side of the ship, a hole where someone's swum under with a poleaxe.

You're just trying to frighten me. That sound's been breathing since the fishes swam, since the sun came up on your quartermaster Smith telling his story. You don't hear anything.

They're sharpening their cutlasses on each other's cutlasses. They'll be over the side even sooner and sharper. We have to go first.

Some ship must've seen you take mine.

Water's seeping into the side of the ship. We're going to have to swim for it.

There's no one in sight.

Only the Malagasy swim, with their daggers in their mouths, and so jolly the rest of the time.

I'll tell them I was taken by force, I'll say I never did what pirates do except that you would kill me if I didn't. Let's hide.

You landlubbing coward. Take this pig knife. It will make a pike if you lashed it to the mop with a length of line and twist the line double. We'll board them first, as quick as they show themselves.

With all the cutlasses you save for yourself, you'll soon be safe and lifting grog in Marseilles, impressing the women with your pirating.

Stop kicking at the door. They'll think you've been hung and never come out. You have to make it sound like happiness. A jig. Like this. Dance the way you danced with Cap'n Peters' girl.

I never knew you could pick up your feet like that.

Ma could, when she wasn't practicing to dangle. Or when she dangled. The fiddler knew.

Let's wave the white flag before we stain it with our own blood, let's tell them Luggams made us do it and show them Luggams. If I hoist this—

Keep your shirt on.

Before I die, let me show you the bone I carved on the voyage out, bought with the last of my money. "Man Sawing at a Tree on the Occasion of His Betrothing."

The title is bigger than the piece.

Aye.

Don't break the door down. Someone is as liable to come through with a plate of brisket as with a knife.

We're the plate of brisket. Don't you see? We're the tasty chum and that's why they've left us up here, to draw them out. I think the deck leans. They're counting the powders and purses below.

These coves we're passing do stink of the Spanish or at least of a Moor tied up in them, burying treasure by the chest as if it were a crop. I say, two boats in a week! What luck!

Hullo! Over here! Bring them on!

They come on like flies.

I'll clean the foredeck with this fork. You get the others up out of their coffins belowdecks—let them fight to their ends and not ours.

Hours Later

12

Get up now and quit your moaning. Best we mop the deck with the blood of the others.

My leg.

Get up, I say. I think we're the last. No one else is looking alive.

Leg.

You can move that leg. You can, I saw you move it when that Moor went after you.

See his cutlass, how it shines—it shines like a jewel in a jar.

Move your leg.

Tomorrow. See the light on the edge of it?

I'll move your leg myself then.

My leg!

Don't scream. Give me your kerchief to stop the blood. And your cutlass.

Not the one I wrested from three brigands and a captain with just your pigknife held between my teeth?

Magnificent, you were. So fierce their eyes didn't blink but you had them shaking. You slashed and slashed. I wondered where you found your piracy so quick, it must be in the family. Now, give me the cutlass.

You'll have my own knife at your throat, you will, just like I had the captain with it.

Want me to pull out the bits from your leg with just this pig knife and my fingers? There be holes in the sail and gulls in the rigging and dead men rolling the deck in their blood, and you won't loan me the use of your cutlass to save yourself, however it was obtained?

So long as I can see it.

You'll feel it.

Wait, wait—where is it going?

There's coals left from the cannonwork—I must burn you to stop the blood.

No, no, not that.

I can slip the cutlass from your fingers after all your insides have rotted. A fine cutlass it is too, with those rubies in the hilt, or is it all my brother's blood?

It's my foot I can't move, nothing's wrong with my leg. This foot is stone.

Watch the flame, watch the flame.

Why can't I faint like a girl?

Just breathe steady instead of making all that noise. Bite the rope like it was Ma's, served up in the soup, and breathe.

I'm bimmm-fff-iiii-ttt-ing.

Leave off me with your bloody chops, you cur. Bite the rope, not me. Already so much blood slicks up the wound I can hardly get a grip on it and I've still got the sawing to do.

I'm fainting, I'm going to faint.

Then faint, in Christ's blood, faint.

I can't.

Stop that screaming, someone will hear.

They're all dead.

Are you sure? They could be like us, they could be resurrecting and fit to kill, or a half-dead cook with his knives.

What—you go wiping the blade on your sleeve like I'm a bloody joint of lamb?

The lice won't stick if I drag it across me clean. If I douse it with water, the sharks swarming will come. Breathe when I do. Breathe.

Breathe, breathe—where did you get a knack for this breathing and butchering?

Bother. The shot is too far in.

You'll cry if I die.

From joy to be rid of you! Sing out or talk, your shrieks make the cutting hard.

O, the merry old man of Bis-do-bee!

Better.

I dreamt of a mermaid the size of a whale with a place to move around inside her, a pleasure place.

Really? Maybe I dreamt it too and didn't tell you. There's the shot. Now, hold still. This blood is so bloody slippery.

Give me that cutlass! Give it to me! You'll do me no more harm.

I'll knock you in the head with it, I will.

The cutl—

Egad, I will have to chop the whole of the leg, to the joint and around. You'll not be thanking me for this. Use the courage you swore to when Luggams made you the pirate you didn't want to be.

My head. You didn't have to crush my brains out!

Now to the coals again.

Coals!

Just a quick burn.

My leg.

As soon as I have you trussed, I'll toss the leg over and goodbye, just like that. Goodbye in the dark and good riddance. Then I'll steal the bo'sun's false leg if he hasn't rolled off, and make you a new one, bye-the-bye, to fit. A leg you can jew up a dance on the spot for the ladies—but hold still now and stay quiet and quit that bleeding.

Four hundred gold pieces?

If there be a pirate left to pay you for the leg. The ship be ours now, and all its little treasure to split between us. There's a squall in the dark that's coming for us, but the sails still be strong. We could be in for a flip.

The ship's leaning on her shoulder already, the fish will be climbing my boots by dawn.

Boot.

Aye, the one.

13

The ship sails itself.

Days Later

14

Having to haul the fly-besotted enemy overboard, it's another offense against us.

They could've left the charts.

They could've left the sails unslashed, the rigging primped and the rudder sound.

Where are we? We'll never see our shores again in this drift, unless we are taken and hanged.

Hanged.

Will you shut that parrot up?

Hanged.

Hold the beak.

The governor himself sat with Shanks and Luggams, and refit their ship in sight of Boston harbor. I heard the mate tell of it.

Home is not Boston harbor.

If we could but steer home.

It's not so far off when it comes to measuring from sea to sea.

A visit home is your grave day.

O'Maury, O'Mallory, they grow their own crosses—
They sit on the shore a-counting their losses

The lassies come begging with boils on their –
And still you keep dancing
And still you keep jigging
Praising the glory of the Cutlass King's lashes.

You made that up.

I made it up while Luggams slept, and sang it in my sleep while he forbade it. I love to sing. I learned from Ma's husband, the sixth.

Hanged.

You know, in another week, I'd have had a solid gold cutlass. We were going up against the King of Cutlasses in a week, the great pirate of España with his knives of gold.

Soft knives, that, in solid gold.

Oh, yes, he would have been our next except you had to practically bleed to death, wriggling round the deck like a briney shrimp, chasing me with your leftover leg.

Shrimp, never.

Hanged.

I've heard of a parrot that could recite all the rivers in Africa.

There's enough talking between the two of us.

But if you were to—

I'm not dead nor drowned in the drink yet.

Tis' a fine leg I made for you, yours is. It's the table that's not much anymore.

I fear my stump is spoiling. Even the spoils you took are spoiled.

That ham they had!

The velvets stood up with mold.

I look nice enough in them, my stitchery done best without the wash of blood.

Butchery, not stitchery.

Hanged.

Shut up! Shut up! I can't stand it.

Our dead foe taught it, to lash himself with warning.

"Save the cook" is better. That's what I'd teach it. Every time before I stick someone, I ask Cook? first, not brother.

A spate of brothers and all of them like you, with your time pieces a'rusting, and foul, desperate boats.

Hanged.

Brothers all, brothers who will make you drink seawater soon enough.

You knew that would bring up the pearls. They were all I had from two years of repairing watches. Now all I have is my leg, the lost one, swimming beside the ship. Would that it would guide us.

By the by, you are free now. Free of the pirates' hold.

Free to die? I swore, didn't I?

Hanged. Hanged.

It's a smart one, to fly off so fast as that.

You should never have released it.

It's taken such a liking to you. Pretties your shoulder.

Begone! Begone! It's just waiting to see if I die of my

leg. A bird of prey.

The game then, before it returns.

Black teeth—Queen of spades.

Blind eye—My deuce.

Nine o' hearts—Pegleg.

Bit pecker—Double sixes.

Fiver—Hook hand.

Pieces o' eight.

You win.

At least the bleeding's stopped.

Pull down the canvas to shade me. I hate all fish though I could swallow a white-fleshed one now, I could.

Hanged.

It's just come back to check on your leg.

Hand me the poker. With the cutlass and the redhot poker, I've got twice the chance of killing it.

Take care, your leg's not—and the wallow of the boat—

Never mind the leg. I'll get it, I'll get it. It's not so high that I can't—with this poker—

Watch out! The deck there—the rope—

Once more—I'll get it sure this time, I will—If I have to hear its gallows' talk once more, I'll—

You missed by a length.

I'll throw this belaying pin at you too, I will, if you don't stay quiet. I think I nicked the wing of it. A nick and a jab, it was, and a good one with the poker. You don't see the bird now, do you?

I don't see the poker neither.

I would sleep but the pain—every wave jolts it—I can't abide the pain in my leg. Or what it once was.

Calm yourself. You're bleeding again.

That is not the death smoke that the priest makes, smoke traveling from the far yonder of the boat?

Not incense, no. But smoke it is. Where did you throw that damned hot poker?

Not far enough, not overboard. I can see the fire rising.

1723 Desert Island

15

I love an island.

I love an island with a bit of wood on it.

Yes, we could use a bit of wood, deserted and empty as it is.

With my leg burnt to ash, I think of wood more than you, I ponder quite a bit over wood.

I would have paddled my own soul to heaven and back for you to get at the wood of our skiff but it drifted. I pressed hard at the oars but our boat stood still with you screaming Fire! of your leg.

I was afeared you had forgotten me.

It was enough to drag your sizzling leg ashore with that cutlass trying to drown us both. Who could see the bloody shore for the smoke of the boat burning and your leg? I couldn't. I was glad for the island, happy for dawn at last.

It's not just the dunes, the dunes suck down the prince of legs, it's this stick I suffer forward on, this twisted length of rotten driftwood you think is so bloody perfect.

You wouldn't want a leg of palm. The Queen's ton it would be. Real wood will float in from the boat. Just wait.

I'll crawl from one end of the island to the other, from leeward to windward, that's my waiting. Cannibals wait, I can't.

You are an idiot.

Tis true. Soon enough a lost shrike or a pigeon or that Hanged will come flying over the island and instead of eating the seed in its beak like a glutton after all its flying for days and days with nothing at all for food, it will drop its seed over a soft patch of sand where the seed will take root and sprout and then branch over our heads to make a place for the gluttonous bird to rest in after all his flying for days and days. Just for me a fine leg will be grown from the tree which we'll then saw down in great haste, having waited as we must, fully for twenty years, but having eaten the bird some years back.

Sea almonds! Wherever I step.

I thought they were stones of a rough sort, hampering my way like every anthill and crack.

Your cutlass could break them open if I could but use its rubied hilt or its broadside.

It is all I have, in protection—and to practice my carving. We must get a gull to drop these almonds from high onto a rock.

You'll be buttering gull on toast in heaven before it obliges us with that great trick. Your cutlass. Now.

I'll run you through first.

You are such a pirate.

I am a legless man in distress. Stand back!

Try for a button on the first mate's canvas or the lace and underthings of McDougall fast across my chest. Come on.

Bless my cutlass, you are such a sight swimming in all

those clothes. They are barely dry.

McDougall was really the one for fancy clothes, always pawing through the chests. I heard him say he was careful not to shoot through the actual hearts of the well-dressed gentlemen so as not to ruin the lace at the front.

At least it's cloud season on this island, and cool for all this you are hauling on your body like it was all you had.

It is.

Hanged.

Mercy!

It liked the fire, it warmed itself by the flames.

Get thee away from me.

Egad.

That was fair close. I swear upon my gobspit that island birds eat more than others, they have that much more to drop.

Make yourself calm. The bird is gone.

I'll play calm when there's no more wave. What? The print of a hand?

A print of a hand.

A cannibal's for sure.

Or a monkey's. There's the palms here for them.

The belt of the earth is higher than this, and monkeys winter in places warmer, or I would.

No footprints, just these marks of a body dragged behind. Another like you, legless.

We must find and succor him!

And share rations? The sea almond splits only in two. You were right, it must be a cannibal's.

Hanged.

Oh, why couldn't we be put ashore according to the rules, with a loaf of bread, a bottle of wine and a pistol with one load? Why did we have to burn and sink? Why this bird—

When the rain comes, you'll catch it in your mouth in the midst of your caviling. Me, I'll find a cup in a shell.

To the cannibal then, we'll toast him.

16

So—the hand was yours. Why, why, why do you follow us? We're but lost lads ruined from greed with nowhere to go even if we change one island for another.

I chase you best through water.

Without your cane you will not gain on me here on land. Except that we are marooned. But for a drink of water, I could use the water.

Rest your wants. The parrot knows the way to fresh water—that's why you should heed it.

My brother will kill the parrot first and drink its blood.

Tell him the cannibal sent it and if he lets it out of his sight, it will squawk to the cannibal of his fire.

He thinks the cannibals are roasting his leg. Every night he wakes screaming that the other leg's gone and bades me to touch it. For him I concocted a salve from a plant as I cut from the shore. Except for the bird, he is better.

I'm sorry that the bird recites "Hanged" so willfully. He must have been cheap, that's all I can say, with a teacher not so skilled as I. I would have taught him "Water."

Oh, for a lime! Get us off this island now, we are bound to this sand and tree and its almonds. Oh, but for a few fish.

All I can do is follow and wait until you will follow

me. Our father despises you every day for not choosing the sea, for locking yourself to the land. Feel around your neck.

I have no gills if that's your meaning.

The mixing of the races does not always come true. Pity. But the sex is always sure. You're my sister.

Don't touch me there.

After Peters caught me, I sang the wrong pirate off the gallows. When first a creature like me comes up out of the deep, all humans and time are alike. I knew you to be a pirate, just not where. After you slipped me your brother's name signed by you, I knew you better. Except you were male. Show me your females.

I will not.

I will swim beneath the poop deck.

Not that! It is hard enough.

Together we will tell Father you have returned.

I know nothing about this father. Leave me be.

He is the father you seek. Didn't your mother tell you?

My mother told me of many fathers, none wishing death upon me.

Although Father is not weighed down by gold and other appurtenances, just by the fishy depths, the pirates so often cannot keep their ships afloat even on sunny days and their treasure sinks to him of their own accord.

All of that treasure is his?

And yours, by way of family, with the squabbles that attend it.

I can't breath underwater.

You haven't tried. Gill/girl. It's just a slip in the writing. Let me teach you exactly how they come together.

Oh, no—that's a lesson I don't want.

Two sister fish we are, and one knows the ways of the shore and can sing a sailor to the very brink, and one trails her hair the way they do, until it catches a sailor.

I have heard the singing when I press my ear to the hull. I have heard my own.

A pirate sees the hair in the tide before he swings, a true wild swag of it. He has to sing back quick or his nether part will grow longer and longer with him a'dangle on the rope. We are uncommonly clever about a man's parts, as you will be too. You must come with me, for the love of our father who abandoned you because he could not stay.

The world is scarce of love, it washes few and drowns most of those.

You will not come?

There it is—the rain at last. I must race to the shells I have collected and nurse my brother.

You are bound to your brother as fast as husband to wife.

Don't come upon him or he will think he is raving for sure and I will have to attend his supporations all over again. And don't leave any more of your prints. He will become a cannibal himself if he is reminded.

You send me away after all my trouble? Why can't you see that you know your rightful place all along, and long now to swim there?

I am no girl, nor fish. I am not your sister, nor your father's child. I am a pirate on a pirate's island, with no past at all, and surely no future. Do not slander what little I have left. Begone from me. Leave my sight!

17

In the beginning, everyone lived beside water.

I like that. Beside and not in it.

Everyone lived beside water that was sweet and you could drink all of it. You didn't wait for a storm, you didn't wait for a bird to show it to you.

Water, I want water.

You should not have scared the bird.

Let it fan me with its water-love, let it fly to me with a key to water around its green neck. I didn't mean to throw so many rocks.

Sit down, sit down. The dew can be sucked from the leaves on the morrow. Let us try again for a water story: Tataunga, the great chief—

—whose teeth crushed shells, who cannot see his business his belly is hitched out so far, who keeps pirates behind staves to dance on his fire.

The savage king Tataunga gives a great feast in praise of water, with grog and beers and soups—

Not soup. Never soup again. Too much rope in the soup.

Tataunga possessed two beautiful daughters, begot by a woman flung off a maharajah's vessel.

Named Ma.

They are all named Ma who have you as a son.

One of the daughters escaped the evil Tataunga and the other stayed below and kept her fins. The son who is not so beautiful is from another father.

So many fathers. What of the fish woman?

She's a whale. Small, but not perch or something with silver in its skin.

Whale, fish—they are all mostly water.

O, hateful water, oh beautiful water.

This beautiful fish with watery fins and skin the color of ruby beaches at sunset the boy befriends, speaking to her just long enough to get her true secret.

Many palms sway behind Tataunga as he dances— what secret would that be? The secret of life? I know that secret, it's the thing that Tataunga does at night to his last and final daughter.

No, not at all. The fish gives him the secret of death instead, that's it, the fish tells him how death fights us.

We are all dying. Great gasping breaths, the hawking, then the phlegm. How can we listen?

Don't lean on me so—the daughter possesses an eye that sees beyond all others and she uses it. Though Tataunga sends her to every part of the sea, to every shore that the seas wash up to find her sister and her secret, he dies before he hears it.

I have the eye. See—a whale's eye.

Give it here. That eye is mine.

I was given it, I didn't take it from you and I need it

now, to fight off Tataunga with mine eye.

It stinks. You don't want it.

I've had it too long to stink, unless it be the stink of my skin against all these washed-up clothes.

Keep the eye then, you cur. Tataunga brings his hooks and axes. I see him bury himself inside the whale's chest.

I'll bury myself.

You'll get sand down your gullet, you'll choke on it.

You are without respect! Tataunga comes to cut out your tongue.

Put down that cutlass. It's my cutlass.

The palms wave as if to attack, we must fight Tataunga.

All right, we'll fight the palms so they don't cut out your tongue. As long as you don't harm the stick I walk on. Tataunga!

Tataunga! Not so close. I think you are too close.

The battle ends with Tataunga drinking a cup of grog with us—

—and weeping over his lost daughter.

What about the daughter?

His tears fall upon the lost daughter and they turn into treasure, pieces o' eight in bags of silk.

Finally, treasure. Which Tataunga doesn't need or want so we hasten to take it.

But you are Tataunga.

I thought you were the daughter.

The fish?

I am not the fish either. I am not even the whale. The secret! The secret! I'll cut it out of them.

Let me seize that sword of yours. You'll do yourself harm.

My eye! You have cut mine eye! You have poked out my eye!

Don't—scream—so.

My eye, my eye!

It's just the one, you can do all your looking with the other.

Get away. Get away. My eye!

Hold it with your thumb to stop it bleeding.

Monster!

We'll get you a patch, a lovely patch out of hide, or a black swatch. It's not like losing another leg.

What am I to do? I'm blind.

You are the one-legged brother who creeps, and now you will have to creep alongside me.

Curse Tataunga and all the Higher Powers!

It's a blessing is what you must think—your one eye will see what comes next where two cannot, they are too busy conferring.

You dream that. What would I see?

A man with a fork rising from the sea to take out the other.

Mercy!

A Year Later

18

I don't know how you see anything through your one eye.

It's a ghost boat yonder, or nothing. It's a boat that floats for sure, that's all.

—A square-rigger?

A true boat, and it coming toward us!

Indeed.

Let's flap our rags, let's jump from a tree! Fire! The fire! Coax up the fire!

No time. They'll be ashore before we can find enough kindling. Besides, they'll never stop if we look like brigands drying our takings over a fire.

Southbound.

Southbound will be fine. Southbound will be just dandy.

Southbound it is. And a big fine ship it is. The newest of sails, all rigged right.

The bones of the burnt hull lure them.

How will they see us?

They see us, they're tacking.

We are but two castaways from a boat caught in the rocks and burnt, that is our story—ah, what was the name of the vessel you heard was refitted?

The *Mayflower* or the *Maryflower,* some-such.

We are two castaways from the *Mayflower,* all that was left of the hundred of your countrymen accosted by brigands and left for dead after the burning boat catched on the rocks.

The flag is English?

It is. But the tale of being beset by something like the Frobisher ship is better, with its fraud so long ago of saying they were looking for the Passage, poking about and picking up women and not discovering—everyone knew Frobisher was a pirate. We begged to be put off the Frobisher-type ship and die here, rather than go on with the likes of that kind of captain.

Pirates like to leave a captain. I vote for the *Mayflower.* The less piratical our boatsmen the better.

Oh, bother—the *Mayflower* or the *Maryflower* then. Move your hand from the glass, you hide the sight of the crew. A monk's on deck—see his cowl?

He will be kind to us.

Unless it's a Moor in disguise. I can't tell from those robes.

If only I had mine eye.

They need water enough, with a barrel like that.

I've forgotten what happened to my leg.

You fell into a well behind the topiary, the topiary behind the—what, what?—it comes to me—the chapel at Edgerton. Your eyepatch is from a fight between us when we were but infants. Which is true more or less since we're naught but boys now. Big orphan boys.

It's a fine thing you're still so light of beard. They like it when there's a woman. That frill off MacAdam's cuff does the convincing. And the skirt from the washed up trunk.

Hanged.

It can't be. I dreamed feathers flying into the dark of the night, it didn't die, it came back. I should've eaten it long ago.

Leave it be. It found us water.

Hanged.

It led us to the brink first.

We must boast that the parrot will find a port, that it was the best of luck for us having tamed it.

Not in all the water of the seas I have drunk will that parrot be luck for us. Damned bird.

Hanged, hanged.

Which of the clothes to put on top for me?

Plaid, it's plaid, a bold plaid it is. There may be some who fled Scotland.

I shall go all enraged—I was all set to land at a new port for the time-pieces when the pirates o'erpowered my ship. But I need a paper that says you took me. I don't want to complicate the road we are set on by not having the right history.

But it would declare me a pirate!

Yes, well, maybe we would surprise them better as two warring sides.

Better we double our forces and turn on them just as they turn the key in your lock.

You were fighting athwart the boat in defense of me.

Hanged.

Get the bird off my shoulder.

I'll stuff it inside your shirt for a heaving bosom.

Ah, yes, that could fool them.

And hide my cutlass under your petticoats on a belt around your leg. They won't think of you with such a weapon. Or should I be carving the wood with it: "The Fine Maiden Hurries to the Dock for Communication from Her Lover?"

No, I will act as a kind of closet for the cutlass. Then after all the introductions, I will fall in a faint in the excitement so you can cover my face and carry me on board with all those weak lady excuses they make. Then we'll poke them.

I'm bound into being a pirate.

It is our best chance. Over here! Over here! We've been besieged by cannibals daily.

Don't say that—they won't land.

They all like to say they've killed the cannibals in defense of the ladies. Hope they don't confuse us with them though. But cannibals have far more teeth than we show. Please—mind the rocks. The rocks are what caught us—the great boat the *Maryflower*—

The *Mayflower*—

The *Mayflower,* god rest our ship and all the souls upon it, it was cast onto the rocks and there met its fiery end. Here! Over here!

The rocks caught us but they've spread for you due to

97

the flag you're flying. Delighted to have you come ashore.

Hanged.

Miss Hanged, if you please.

19

You are no monk.

Zee cut of zee monk's jib iss zo cool for zee nethers. But you—you are no uzual caztaway!

My sister, Monsieur.

Miss Hanged, if you please. Daughter of the First Magistrate of Barbados.

A lovely ranzom for zee daughter of Julian Julien, zee castrated cur of the Carribbean.

I was got out before he was maimed.

Aye, well, I don't doubt that he had zome meanz about him. Give Miz Hanged and her bird the, the how-do-you-say? cloizter where she might go pale in the arm and the faze so as to fetch a better huzband in zee first zlave market we come to, or persuade Julian Julien zhe is worth a virgin'z ranzom. White as zee znow you will be by zen, and a big enough purze for uz, like az not. And find her a fine comb of fizhbone got from her father, the fine caztrated Julian. Adieu, mon cheri, I will veezit you zoon, zo zoon. Az for her having a brother—Julian Julien muzt have led a buzy youth.

Hanged.

I am a watchmaker of some repute. M'lady knows—

Zilence. Do not zpeak of Miz Hanged. We are not

talking about zee father of zuch a woman. Perhapz we should be talking of parrotz.

I am not even English, I am from Salem, from another father.

Comme si comme ca, zneaking puppy of the colonies. Back to your ztationz, the rest of you. I don't want to zee the lay of the land, I want to zee zeez one's zkin.

I swear to you!

Sacre bleu! Zuch a young one. Zo fine a zkin for zuch a pirate'z back. You will learn the wayz of the flesh—mine.

Five lashes only! I cannot take more than five.

The lash lovez you. The lash lovez and lovez the one-legged—

Only ten!

Yez, yez, yez. Oh, yez. We will zee how many.

No more!

Hanged.

Only after a pirate haz zeen the lash can he be trusted. Bligh, take heem below—and have the leg looked after by zee carpenter, zome paint applied. When zee lucky zailor recoverz from hiz lashes, he can inflame me with a leg as zhapely as hees zeester'z. And ztow the unbozomed bird in my quarterz.

A Week Later

20

I try to throw up my skirts.

It is hard to distract him. Just the sound of my pegleg upon deck and he comes at me again with his lash.

He calls me his bête noir.

Isn't that one of those little cakes? He is stupid not to force you or we would be dead and at the bottom of the drink, both of us, from your lack.

They had dugong the week before.

"Zee fair mermaid of zee zea." He has taken you away so often to "heez zuite" it's hard to believe he has not tired of the farce.

I keep him off with stories—how boats will sail underwater by the power of cannonballs, one ball smacking the other, of the prince who cuts off his finger and a new prince grows from it, of the mermaid who sang to the wrong man—you know, whatever I can twist together.

We would still be swanning the decks if the parrot hadn't flown from your bosom and ruined our Mayflower story. And the magistrate had to be impotent! Spending so long on that island even the gossip goes green. But the shackles are the same.

At least I don't have to bear them on my ankles. It would be hard to sneak down with their clink, clink, clink.

If I ever get hold of a cat o' nine tails—

You sound pirate enough now.

Aye, I'll cut that parrot down first, and then the rest of them too. Avast ye, and the like.

Where can we escape to? The swells are high enough without us.

See the paleness in me.

Pale as a pirate's turnip.

Bother. Let's talk of the soup they kept in the Turk's Head pot, across the gibbety square, the fine bones and mustards we never ate as pirates.

We're in the soup now.

It is rough today.

Everyone else in chains goes aboveboard but you.

I don't want to go up. There's Silas and Fremont, dead of the fever and if the Frenchman finds them, I'll have to haul out their bodies and my wrist is finished, a bloody stump from these shackles. I might as well get a hook now and be done with it.

You should not have got your hand caught in that loop of rope.

I was trying to grab for his faretheewell when he walked down with his whip, and my peg tripped me. But what of you? You're a gimlet-eyed false woman with your fineries so fair, so many castoff jerkins you look about to birth a nation of castaways.

They do round me. He lets me keep them all, even the lacy bits.

No more talk of the Frenchman. Let's talk of women,

the women of my wants, the women in my life.

The harridan, your wife?

She made me drink quince at every meal and diced my socks with rough yarn. There is nothing like that kind of a woman to suck you down.

The anchor that pulls you under.

The woman we courted, now there was a woman.

Aye. A pirate's woman before we were pirates.

I daresay she had an eye for you in my dazzling wake.

An eye, yes, but not a foot. She didn't stray from your path.

The last woman I heard had a tip-tap so light on deck it could have been a goat.

It was a goat. You could smell it roast for hours.

Not food, not so much food in our talk. Me-hearty me with a song if you must. My wrist!

Avast ye, creature of Ma-a-a-mmon,
Bail ye, swine, past long lost Adam—

You rhyme without shame.

I hate this belowdecks of yours and my getting pale for a slavers' auction. Let us talk of fish instead, of the fish swimming alongside us, a'singing.

That was a swell, no fish song.

They sing what fools we be, you a scrimshaw saint, I a dead mother's helpmate.

Your foot is in my hair.

I thought it was vermin!

The fish sing that the wind is upon us now. The fish, the wind—they sing together.

Your bowels are so loud I can scarce hear myself.

Now a scratching only, a fish come to gut us from below.

21

All hanz on deck! Methinz zee ship is zinking or I have fallen into me glasz! Where is zee crew?

Washed over or strung out on the line, shackled and drowned behind the boat.

I zay drink to zee drowned then! Where is the plug to plug ziss hole?

Lightning green on the rigging, the spar's loosed up on deck, and the waves—

A fairy show. Evil faireez. I have seen fish standing on the wavez to greet uz, fish big as zaintz. To zee wine eenstead, zwill a drink to the cutlass by ze Savior de Papa, as ze Portuguese would zwear it!

Hanged. Hanged.

Which way, parrot?

Zee parrot knows zis lightning. Drink to zee parrot.

The wheel's tied off.

Itz spokes cried out for the rope! By my gown of zee Christian monk and the gown of Meez Hanged and zee bold waters of Julian Julien—

Well done! He needed the crucifix as hard as you gave it.

The gash won't kill him. Another wave!

I thought you'd washed over with the rest.

I hate the deck so, I stayed clear of it when they halloed.

Oh, god let us stay afloat.

Another.

That's the mast going. Take his sword—it is yours, the rubied one. Fasten yourself to it.

The lash, I want the lash too.

Leave the lash, you idiot.

Waves across the fo'sicle, waves that—

Took the lash.

Yo-ho-ho, yo-ho-ho, yo-ho-ho.

Drink his drink down. All of it. It'll hot your gullet, quiet your bloody bones, it'll settle you where you need settling.

Argh!

His blood rushes out as quick as the water rushes in.

Hanged.

I'll cut off the beak of it!

Enough slaughtering.

No wind of a sudden.

Clear as Christchurch! The sky scrubbed rough with soap.

This could be but the eye, just the eye of the storm.

I've heard tell of it.

We'll swim home.

Don't dance in the rigging yet. I'll climb the crowsnest.

Maybe we are drowned and don't know it. The blue-painted ocean—who said that? Why do you dally so?

Don't tip the flagon so deep. Wait until I make my report.

Report?

It's a trick of the weather up there. Is there a rope yet to belay me?

Under that cask that is split.

I don't see a cloud in all of the sky, not a one.

My stump be a'tingle, how can it storm more?

We'll need real luck this time. The parrot—

—left its feather.

I'll take a drink now. What—just the dregs?

If the wind comes, athwart is where I'll be the safest. I'll lie down there.

It's black above now, you drunkard.

There's a face at the scuppers, a dead slave come to haunt us. Oh, god from above!

A woman?

They say they come at the last.

Only a screaming wind and more wave.

Best we lash ourselves down.

Yes, the deck at last.

Not both of us to one plank or we'll both go to heaven.

One for both, or none. No swimming for me.

Nor for myself neither.

The wind! The wind!

Come away from the side. The heaving's less here, hold to the hatch.

The heaving's worse, the wine—I'm—

All over me.

22

I saved you.

I thought the fish saved me.

That terrible fish? It was as big as the size of yourself and roiled through those waters like two men, it was as big as the water pigs Bligh told us of.

Must've come up from the deep on account of the storm.

It had you afloat on its scales until I came at it with my cutlass. I couldn't see its face—

You stuck it with the cutlass. Almost through the gills.

Gills or gullet, I couldn't see for the thrashing. Waters like hell, they were. It had ahold of you and you were going full to your end, going down, down, down in all your many clothes.

My pockets will drown me yet.

Take out the coin next time.

I had no coin. I saw other fish circling, while it had me.

Not I.

Others came up around it in the swirl of the blood and the storm.

You did not see that. You were too soon holding fast to my leg and blowing to the surface.

I saw what I saw. The fish was less holding me than pulling me down as sure my leg now dangles for the sharks to trim.

I saved you with my wooden leg afloat.

If the wind hadn't fallen, we would have been finished, wooden leg or no.

The wind fell.

The wind is falling more now.

Falling.

Falling.

The water is cold and will be colder—this current sweeps north.

More boats north.

The waves will decide, boat or not.

So soon? What ho?

Those rogues never turned our way before, unless to gull us. Stay low.

Let's hullo them.

No—wait for a sign—

We should wait while sharks and the other fishy demons eat off our last three legs?

We should. That's Smith at the bow, that villainous grogman, the keeper of the stories of brothers Bungleston and of pirates pale as turnips. From Luggams' crew.

Friend or foe? I don't remember.

Friend, friend—I don't know. Someone we know.

You two, whatever you be doing in the drink swimming like the fish knew your names? Get on aboard and rest your fins.

23

What happened to your face?

Lightning.

It was not lightning. As true as I am the Reverend Baltrick and have run before many a sail on the open seas, never have I seen what I saw with Smith. It was a fish that hit him. It flew up and hit him across the nose on his way up the mast that last day we were becalmed off the Cape. A plague of fishes such as the Bible speaks of had flown onto the boat, even into his pockets and down his shirt. They flew in from all the heavens and one hit him.

Poor fish.

Aye, Smith even found fish in his bed a day or so later, didn't you, Smith?

As you say it, Reverend. But the lightning did it.

He smelled to heaven.

I say it was lightning, Saul's true lightning, that mess of fish coming at me in the air, the Lord's will. The Lord knows. He sent a fish flying up out of the sea a'flapping to my face as sure as lightning.

The Lord? Is this the Smith that sailed the seven seas with Luggams and myself?

Yea, I be that Smith. And this be your brother from the takings?

Aye, and a fine pirate my brother was after he was hauled.

True pirates, drinking the sea in shifts, hanging onto that leg for hours.

Pray, put thy swords and the small knives in the chest there and drink some of our wee grog to stop your shaking from the cold of the deep. The cutlass chest is eight paces hence, more or less, put it there. That's it.

Mind the pegleg.

Why, our thanks to you, Reverend Baltrick. The grog is good, not the burnt peas we drink that slavers make.

Well, we be not slavers. Have no fear of that. And no blow will sink us because we have cleared the sucking sump of the gates of hell and are bound over the farthest seas in Our Lord's name back to our port. But now I must see to changing the course. Smith, thou wilt stand watch.

Baltrick, Baltrick—I believe I heard our mother speak of this Baltrick.

Could he be the Baltrick of the Heaven Sent, the preacher of the Seven Seas she did once have the acquaintance of, as they say?

This Baltrick knows no women.

None? Not even in the seeds of his youth? Our mother swore on her deathbed—

Reverend Baltrick is not the man of your mother's bed, death or not.

Our mother did swear of many.

You have his very eyes, brother.

You can see that, with your one?

What are you two whispering?

We have much to be grateful for and thank the Reverend indeed.

The Reverend has it that you must attend the rigging now, with my help. There's a loop that is bent wrong from the blow.

I'll take the halyard.

So, Smith, how did you come into this service from Luggams'? To my memory, you left his boat just before we were wrecked.

It was just a matter of shifting my doss, you know, when nobody was looking. After Luggams came to nothing and a bad doubloon, owing to the fine crew he shipped, I quit him for a tighter lot. That is to say, I sail now for the Lord Almighty straight out of Boston Harbor even on the blackest of days, and in storms, in search of souls.

Our Smith, the pirate? I say it again but I can't believe it.

I rescue pirates and return them to the Bosom of our Lord, or as the Judge sees fit.

Judge?

This one with the leg isn't right, is he? Always wanting to repeat. Has he been lightning-hit as well as me?

He's right enough, Smith. Go on with it.

My task is to steal the heinous souls of pirates back for God and Mammon, and on the occasion of a soul unrepentant or as a judgment against the people, the Reverend here sails them in and then the Judge tries them and hangs them.

For a bounty, of course.

The wise-legged one! He at least knows the cost of saving the souls of pirates for our Savior who both giveth and taketh away the way. Do not worry, we are not so far from land, a day's journey, no more, and you too will soon be taketh away.

Smith!

The storm pulls hard when you have the Lord Almighty coming for you. Belowdecks, now.

We too be saved and sorry, and will be full of joy to abide in the searching for souls with you. Let us enter Boston in triumph, for the judgment of pirates other than ourselves!

It's the eye patch no one will believe. You shan't pass for naught but pirate.

I'll pluck it off and offer my eye-hole.

It's the patch and Boston harbor only a tide away, and the number of pirates we find who are scarce as you hereabouts, except after storms. And, of course, there's the bounty. Stand just here on your pegleg—another point of the pirate.

I'm a watchmaker, not a pirate.

Reverend, they go not willingly to God.

No—not the irons again—

We hoist sail and wash the decks better than most. Our last captain—a Frenchman he was—thought well of our handling of the line. This hook I have be the best ballast for a sturdy knot.

To blows then!

Good for you, Smith—in one strike. But methinks you should have found a better set of shackles in port. What do we go out for if we have only this soft tin—to rescue crippled sailors from their watery grave? Fetch the bit and the cord from the chest.

Not so tight.

Smith's a blackguard, Reverend. I tell you in our sainted mother's name.

Yes, perhaps he seems reformed at hand, but he'll tow you to hell and back for your ship. Whilst ourselves, we are just poor boys afloat, rescued and homeless from the terrible storm.

Quiet, the two of you, or I'll belay you both again with the "hand o' God."

Have pity. We are your sons indeed, sent by and by. Our very mother tells us Baltrick's the one, aye, Baltrick, and we set sail to find him, no reason other than for the recovery of our father.

Prithee?

Oh, father!

Boston Harbor

24

Why did they have to hang Smith in such a dead wind?
Row faster and the stench will lighten. I'll watch the course.

I see nothing but the blasted moon of your back.

Just row and we're bound to hit something.

Baltrick.

Sea wolves and jackanapes! No wonder Ma didn't hold
to him. I'm sure the heat of hate has already set his sail, if not
the stink of Smith, Baltrick's bonus.

Smith always did stink.

He stank up the whole of the colony. The gaoler told
me the surgeons were wanting a try at him, to have a peek
at his heart and suchlike but the gibbet was too soon fouled
by crows dissecting on their own, having a look at the black
heart themselves.

You are a one for disappointing that gaoler. He didn't
like Smith.

I sang when the noose came up.

And what be the tune? I may need it yet.

The song is on my tongue tip, it is there but I can't tell
you, it is gone the way they say it goes. But you can be sure I
didn't stand around trying to catch it again—I ran. Pray, how
did you stall your gaoler's fancy?

With the figures I put into the gaol wall using the spoon butt—"St. Peter Choosing the Keys." My years of practice for the bone repaid me well. For every prisoner the gaoler said he would always get the cleverer, and I was the cleverest of all.

Aye. The burying you told him was.

Oh, but those eight buried silver bars, I say like I have laid eyes on them, even hauled them halfway around the world. Like pirates float to the beach on bars of gold or silver!

That would be a shipwreck.

I made mention to the gaoler of that fresh water running in the glen just outside the town. A right marshy place, I say. Then he tells the hangman I need time to repent and brings me double rations and forgets to close the door quite so hard as before. We be needing a new door for half a year now, he says and he lifts his eyebrows like they aren't his own.

It's the spoon you stole they'll hang you for next time.

It's the ring in my ear.

They have the teeth of pirates is what the woman called out from the hanging crowd. Look at their teeth, will you? They have the teeth of the islands, soft from the cane and the scurvy.

Never trust an innocent girl.

With us still heaving out of the sea. And Smith talking of the Lord as quick as he could.

It was his sister that didn't like him, that was the poxed woman who called out. We did a bit of convincing with Baltrick too.

Just row a bit to my shoulder, I think I see the shine of the sea starting under that slice of the moon.

No. A squid jumping to the light.

These good town fathers chose to have a man hold a red hot iron just for stealing a chicken.

The gaoler followed close on me in the night, with a fat cudgel ready to put me in that hole he was going to dig for the treasure.

I saw bits of his shirt left on the thorn that keeps that harbor so quiet.

You saw him then?

I followed his shirt and stole up behind him and he nearly dropped his shovel, he was taken with me so sudden. I said, Here, I said, I am dead, and I gave the shovel back to him. The silver's ten paces farther, I walked away saying. Pieces o' nine, I heard him say while I turned to find you, pieces o' ten. Like he was counting it already.

We must watch ourselves exact at this latitude or he'll have us on the boil.

Unless he finds O'Henry's chest.

Only O'Henry's own mother knows the whereabouts of that chest and she is carving the rock that is over it with a teaspoon, keeping the leavings in a bag under her skirts. Besides, O'Henry turned Mohammedan before he left Luggams. You can hear him moaning in that part of the marsh, *My foreskin, oh my front piece.*

Stop, stop. I haven't laughed for a week.

It would be enough for the gaoler to find his gaol

empty of the pirate next to be hung, but for the gaoler to be found guilty of the unlawful stealing of a pirate's treasure unlawfully got!

The judge will see to the finding—and then split it.

Maybe there are truly bars of silver buried in there, resting? With the trees, the mud, the easy confluence of drowned sailors and ships and O'Henry moaning in the marsh?

Our ploughed luck. And here's more of it—we might as well be glued to the sand with this leadbottomed skiff of yours, it sits so heavy in the water against a tide like this.

A ship will come along, a better one than before.

There's a tolling now.

Three. Time moved slow waiting for you to come out of the muck before I heard your whistle.

Row to the next cove, there's bound to be a ship there, in such a pirate's drink.

But whose?

Row, just row.

It's a danger—

Wish we were served with Smith's flying fish today. I could eat two raw, still flapping.

Nothing will come along, ship or whale. We'll have to row to Timbuktu.

Hanged.

Egad!

It means we are on the right road.

Like the devil's hawk it is, waiting for me in the

damned true hunger of my youth, fluttering above.

Hanged.

Food, food at last—that's what I hear. Flying swankey.

Row. And row.

Sometimes I think you're happy to have that leg of wood, to trail it beside my rowing and tease the bird.

Oh, many's the time I wanted such a leg, oh, yes. To go with mine eye and hook. Get to your rowing hard. Harder!

Hanged.

Hush, hush—a ship.

It's got Baltrick's prow on it.

You thick-witted, skull-less, one-legged, one-eyed idiot-brother—not so loud!

They must be out carousing.

The boat, hold the boat—Don't hit it again. Where's the line?

Hanged.

Not if the watch is drunk and sleeping.

Let's see what we can take before they take us.

A pleasure to plunder our dear father, be he yours or mine.

25

Beef, beef—and that one that holds the corn—the lightest one's leather. See, the chalk marks?

A little more of the candle and I could see—move the candle thus. Your arm ruins the light—

I hope the watch can't untie your knots.

His head is knots.

Here's a cask about the right size of the ones I heard Baltrick was taking on, though it's not dry. Hear it?

Open it anyway. Gold plates in wine—I've heard that tried. Baltrick's shipwright has a beard that points to mischief in that way. But easy with the cutlass. You don't want vinegar and gold splashing the deck.

What a mess.

Cornmeal—and gold sacrileges, gods of one or the other. You'd know Baltrick would have those.

Maybe a dozen.

Hanged.

The bird will give us away again. I'll catch it in this corner—it can't fly off down here. Just—by the neck.

No!

Like a dream! Not even a squawk. Mind the blood. I'll

skewer the bird to my peg to quiet my walking, that's what I'll do. But first a feather.

You fool you, you fop.

Aye—and you're the pirate.

Not as stupid as you. There's got to be more booty at hand than just gold gods for our sacks, and a handful of feathers. What of this barrel?

If the mallet were here—

Jerk it hard—

It's open, it's open. Move the light close.

For delivery at the dock and right to their Missus' carts, I'm sure. Not spoilt a bit.

Baltrick did like the making of a pickle.

I wonder how O'Henry's head feels about being so close to Flannery's parts. Help me get the staves back.

Do they stay pickled once they put them in the ground for burial? Is it sort of an immortality they give them, unwitting?

Unwitted.

A lot of salt it took.

Salt they have.

Hush. It's someone alive above and looking about.

It's them come back, Grifton or some lug. Baltrick walks like a lord, it's not him.

Grifton's the sort who might kill us if we haven't got gold, as much as if we do. Let's take the gods.

I'll stay below as always.

We must show ourselves, fight or beguile them.

That's my arm you're pulling, my arm where it was lashed and the hook that pulls so.

You come up or you'll end up in a barrel yourself. Mind the blood.

Baltrick!

They must have polejammed him. Guts and more guts.

Hush.

If it's mutiny, whose side should we cast for?

The navigator's. At least then we won't be lost.

III

1728 Arctic Spring

26

Serves him right for wanting his name on a map and not treasure. I've heard of navigators like him but I never wanted to lay eyes on one, let alone drop his anchor.

We shouldn't have left the ship to hunt. The seals were a trick of light, luring us.

Seals was his excuse. He wanted an explore. If only he hadn't dallied, waiting for the clouds to part like some sign.

They didn't part, they parted us from the blasted boat.

The next melt of ice and the boat will hove to. I swear it, he says. But everyone knows the snow falls year round here.

He was headed right off the edge of the earth.

I could feel that through my socket. Some big cataract at its very edge.

First a loud roar, he says, and all the creatures of hell will fly up and push the boat down, all those winged dragons he talked of.

That's the truth of it.

A pleasure to eat him.

It was the parrot that loved us.

A love light on me shoulder. The way treasure is never heavy, the same.

You're an old guff, saying that about a parrot so long gone, and so hated.

It's the change of heat and the company that makes it so. I never thought we'd be anywhere the drifts would come up to my boot.

Nearly all the way to your tinkler, it is.

I wished I had those boots of yours. I take back what I said, that you looked like a dilly on the streets of Yarmouth, I meant to say those boots just cried out for trouble.

What? I can't hear you with the sacrileges clanking.

Trouble, I said. I loved that parrot.

White—white all over.

Worse than a dead ocean on a flat day. Hardly a sea to see in such a snow.

Treasure's not heavy in the heath, not heavy on horseback, not heavy in the hold—but heavy as hell's a'blazes in a snowstorm and heavier still when the snow's all over and boot high.

We must leave it.

But treasure be the point of pirating.

All this time and we had a wont of treasure, yes, yes,

but leave it now we must. The treasure, or your life. That's always the way of treasure.

I wouldn't leave it for an explore and I won't leave it now.

A map, then, for where we finally heave it off.

Think high thoughts, where the snow starts in the heavens—the sacrileges are not so heavy.

The last paper we had was charts.

The navigator burned them soon enough. To get warm, he said but I know he did it so we couldn't get back and say he got himself and us lost.

We didn't eat him at first, did we? We tramped.

He kept coming up.

Froze where he fell. Froze with the ashes of his charts sooting his pantleg.

I'd burn them myself all over again, just a cat's ass warm it would make me, mind you, the way it did.

But don't you remember—you still stand in the clothes of that first wreck as well as the dead of this one—you have paper. If you could be so kind as to review the pockets of Giorno? I went through mine own when you needed a sweet to suck on, as you might remember, and I can tell you right off I haven't a scrap. Giorno had jewels wrapped in paper, I saw him steal them from the diva.

I can't quite reach—

I can bend my hook. Alsop's pockets, full of damp salt herring, Redbeard's with twine—always one for twine for garroting, and here's a shark's tooth from Davy Brown's or else his own tooth, what do you think? And here's that whale's eye.

Don't you ever throw anything out?

I'll be keeping that.

There's a pocket in the rear in these rags of Louis' and they're as empty as they should be for one so prone, Lindamood the Younger's kept rocks, rocks I tell you, that's all he ever wanted. Giorno's jacket was the rubbed blue? You're right, I remember Giorno had paper for toileting, like he was royal. *Candide* he called the pages.

Check that brace of pockets he kept by his belt. My hands are too stiff.

Candide was short, I remember him saying. But there's nothing.

So much for the literary boot.

What about carving a map into your leg, notches that tell the place of the booty-leaving by way of the carving?

Last time it was only three days before we forgot what the marks meant and then the wood splintered and I needed a new leg. You could carve notches into my good leg now, it's as cold and as stiff as wood.

My tongue's bit in pieces.

That's the parrot feather you bit, where it was hanging low to your hat and froze.

It could have been a quill.

No ink but blood.

Oh, for another bird.

Pirates nearly always put treasure somewhere hard to find, it's just hard to find the pirate who can ever find a treasure again.

You've had too much sun in the face.

Look who's talking about sun, with your eye crusted shut and the patch missing.

They're shut so I don't go blind looking at that earring of yours against the ice.

That isn't my earring, that earring froze and tore off at the start. That's the sun itself through the fog that's coming up fast through the ridge we've got to make for.

The fog's running toward us.

Swill, that's what we need. A nice bowl of swill.

A nice warm gallows.

A lit fire under our feet. A map that shows where to go, not so much of where we've been. The next cove or the next.

Oh, for the navigator.

He could read a map and draw one too.

It's not my fault he stepped into the first hole he found in his explore. A man has to watch his feet in the snow.

And not burn the map. At least we didn't go in for that idea of his of roping us together. Where would that have put us?

I do heartily repent.

I repent I did so little mischief.

I was lucky to get a striped shirt to parade about the deck in—though it looked more like prison garb in advance to me.

Always the fashion with stripes.

My sacrileges, my beautiful sacrileges.

Six of them are mine.

Any fool going south will see them thirty miles away when the snow's all melted.

There are no other fools. Besides, the snow will never melt.

You said Carnaby went this way.

Carnaby liked a mirage. Carnaby smoked mussels and hid them in his shoes. I would've liked to have eaten his shoes.

Carnaby never left the boat, the boat we'll never find.

Did the ice eat it?

The ice or the wind or it sailed away.

It could've been in the next cove.

No.

Carnaby'd be the one to find the gold gods, if he were about.

Carnaby hated gold, he only took pearls. I heard him say so. Picky after all his years of plunder.

People coming upon our sacrileges will run to them. A mirage! they'll shout. Like Carnaby.

Or they'll walk the other way, afraid it's the golden gates swung wide. Again I say—Farewell to the gods.

Straight on?

Straight to hell, that's where there's heat.

Where we left the treasure is a kind of monument to us.

We'll be dead by the time someone finds it.

That's the way of monuments. They don't put them up if you're still alive in the world.

Who's to know it's ours if we don't mark it? If we'd made a map, at least we would have marked the booty like an owner with an X. We must go back and mark it.

"*Stiff*" it should be named on the map, after ourselves.

Let us turn around and put the X—

Ahead—there—

What-ho?

Whisper proper now, whisper. We don't want to scare it.

27

I slaughtered it on the spot. With my cutlass drawn so.

It didn't even lunge at you.

I held on. I put my pegleg into the ice, and held on.

It was sick.

I hacked its head off.

Bother your boasting. I'm going inside. Wake me before the slit freezes shut.

Wait—there's room for two if we eat this or that and get rid of the offal, a little more room just there.

This bit's good.

Too bad there's no wood. It's big enough inside for a fire.

Someone would find us if we had a fire.

Someone would save us if we had a fire. It's the rule of the ice.

They'd just save us for later.

I'm colder than you. Pull your leg in and close the gap with the head.

You'll have to unscrew the leg.

It's off. We'll have a nap. It's warm through.

Into the belly of the beast, foot to head, the two of us

about to be birthed into another world not half so—

That was quite a bear.

Not so much white as green. I thought it was a shrub come to life.

Not as green as that.

Mossy.

If you be the back legs, I'll be the front and we'll creep up to a pack of them.

The front paws are frozen dead to the drift.

Pull, pull.

No, sleep, sleep.

Sleep will kill us.

Sleep.

Open the wound as a window.

There. Now the snow is houses-high.

There be no houses here.

Some new snow, as I said.

You forget how much in your sleep. It's no deeper.

We'll sink and be swallowed, we'll need a boat to cross it.

It will harden or it will melt.

What's that coming? Another bear?

Quit your shaking, you with your mighty cutlass.

He wanted our bear.

He wanted a bit of talk.

He wanted to separate us and then slaughter us.

He wanted to get inside.

A South Seas whaler, can you imagine that? A man from the colonies is a rare enough but a whaler from such a place, coming all the way from what they call the Viceroyalty of Peru to here?

Must've been pressed.

Must've been hard pressed.

So all the time you had a paper.

Aye.

Kind of him to read it.

He thought it would save him, I thought it would save me. Baltrick wrote it out, the cur. But instead of it swearing I'd been forced—

It said to kill us.

It were the Black Spot, only with words. I could have read the Black Spot. At least I didn't give it to the gaoler.

You get to your death and it says the same for everyone.

I should have learnt to read words.

And myself!

The paper was very complimentary to my bravery.

He read it wrong.

You're a cagey brother. It shows we are not related, this caginess.

You were looking at me with eyes penny-size whilst his whale-lance whistled through the bear.

His face was at me so sudden.

We had the bear's true likeness with that fur upon us so well and tight, and breathing hard with us going about inside. He was no fool.

Too bad you hit him so hard.

I didn't think so quick as my cutlass.

We could have wanted more of a talk from him.

Aye. A bit more before the dying.

At least he read out the paper.

But he ate the paper.

Must've been hungry. All those weeks he had without what you need, food or a drink of water. Alone.

Put your hat on your head, your nose has gone black.

By the blood of the bear.

That whaler thought you were the almighty himself, with a pitchfork and tails, and that by reading he could get a berth with you, the devil-priest carrying the paper for our hangings.

You'll not remember.

What?

He was our brother. See the ring on his last finger but one? A perfect emblem of the scar on your back.

You'll be seeing brothers in bears next. You are saying we shouldn't eat him?

I am not saying so much as that. I'm saying Brother!

A South Seas pinkie whaler? Ma could do better than that.

Brother!

He would eat you and then me if we had not been so fast. Better we drag the leg of the bear with us for food and keep watch for the boat he left behind him with others of his like. He's not going to spoil.

I'll keep my cutlass clean.

Let's try seven paces forward and then seven west and seven north and fourteen east, each time forcing a distance away from them without returning.

I hope you prove better with numbers than with letters.

Seven's the number, a lucky one. See, we're moving directly in one direction even though we're touching all four of them.

Seven, and seven, and seven. The seven seas. I can do sevens.

And fourteen. Oh, for a cove and the depths.

You did make a pirate, didn't you, after all, brother?

Seven.

Sorry. You have to watch which way. Now I've lost count.

What's this? Did somebody else leave their golden gods out on the ice like a service was wanting? Is this a regular dropping off spot for sacrileges? What could the priests and Beezlebub be thinking? All of them in a nice little row like that, not buried nor mapped neither.

Quiet now, silence. You'll shake the snow off the cliffs.

I have the need to speak as much as you do. South Seas, South Seas.

Spit it out. South Seas! But silent. By the by, isn't that your ear there we saw from the last time around?

The navigator's. Too tough, remember?

Perhaps our boat met the South Seas'. "Two Boats Abraided by the Icy Seas" be the figure.

Aboutface on seven, lips or no lips, I say. We're walking away from them, we're leaving them.

Was that a whole turn or a half?

The wind feels by half.

Yes, that's good. I remember the wind against the gold.

Nothing can scare me after Ma.

Must be death coming on if you're telling me about our old Ma again. Must be death in a hat or all this quiet.

Shshshsh. Someone's abreast of us.

It's gone, whatever followed.

There's always blood to mark the spot.

Only if it were plenty.

You want to kill me to mark it.

I did not say that.

It were on your very lips.

Nothing but ice on my very lips. Let's leave the cutlass instead of blood. Finders would know pirates was here with such a one as yours, with the rubies at the hilt.

You just want me unarmed, you're wanting me to leave it so you can grab it and use it on me and then eat me too, your own brother.

Never. Truly, never. Ach—these lips.

You're not going to bother with a match or some wood like you did the others, you're just going to take my cutlass and stick me to mark the treasure with and then eat me raw and bloody.

Bloody hell.

Give the eye up.

It's mine.

Give it up.

I don't have it.

I know which pocket.

Oh, which?

She was my woman and not no one else's—not Peters' nor yours, you traitor of the seven seas. Brother!

Give me that back, give it to me—

Traitor.

You threw it, you half-a-brother with half-a-leg and one eye and no brain and a hook, with an idiot's stagger and the pirate's want of parts lost out of stupidity and cupidity and titty—goodbye this time for good or ill. Goodbye and nothing. You can find your own way, you can crutch along until your stump goes soft, you jealous slag. I'm away, I'm off, I'm gone.

28

You cast out the whale's eye?

My brother threw it.

He is not your whole brother and you are not the son of the father you think. Here, take it back.

I don't have a father.

Your father floated to the top, and then sank straight to the bottom where your mother has wormed to.

My mother was buried.

There's good water beneath your place, and strong current. Your mother does not fear it anymore. Now, get your foot out of the drift and listen: Your father is dead at last of the cut your brother gave him in the troughs of the storm.

He was the fish we fought?

A man of the sea. The mustachioed man of your mother's Manuel.

Begone, you witch of the sea. Such lies!

But I have your child.

No, no—the child gone over?

The one you birthed from all your clothes.

The boat voted to put the babes and Molly off, for lack of food. I had no choice. I stitched an X to its pocket. I wanted it to have my name at least.

Name, name. Does the minnow bear a name? I was planning a treatise on the names of the healing kelp but no one will read it. They prefer to stare at the sky until the kelp washes over their wounds. Come below now. It's time. Your babe is here.

Not below.

That's the fear in you again, the mother-half that fights the father. How far I've had to chase you! Come now, the ice shifts, it will close again soon.

The water—

The sweet, sweet salt of it.

Can I not rest on your fishy rump and think it out? For a short time at least.

Oh, thinking, that's what you'll do there? Hasn't the fighting of pirates and all the charnel-making chased thinking clear from your head?

It is thinking that makes me live. My true father, dead?

Seven, and seven. To fourteen.

My brother comes, to spite me.

Live then.

29

It must be the cold. You must have seen things. That woman from before? I have but one eye but even I can see this is not the place for such rendezvous.

Seven. And twenty-eight. Wipe that eye of yours better. Night is approaching. I saw her.

Night is not approaching, day is.

Seven.

You should not go off without me, brother.

Aye.

You won't leave me again, will you?

I didn't leave you for nothing, you forced me to go by throwing away my one thing, you brute!

Aye.

Aye.

Do you have a rope?

Am I the child of my mother?

Tie it between us so we cannot part.

Between us? As stupid as that navigator, letting Death have a chance to laugh twice?

I say tie it. I cannot drag my leg on without knowing

you are here with me, talk or no talk.

You'll drag me down.

I'll lead you out. I know the way.

You do?

I have the bravery, I found it after you left me for good, to see things.

Let us keep to the number.

Quit muttering.

That monk—the Frenchman on the boat that slaved us, he muttered to himself too. I caught it from him. He lay athwart the hatch while you were below. Sometimes while he muttered, he worked out a paper from under his robe and folded it.

He had paper?

He would fold it and fold it, this bit of paper, into a gull that flapped.

Seven hundred and fourteen. He made a bird from a paper?

Aye. I saw it, while telling out one of my stories to keep him from lashing you. It flapped, his bird, like life.

You'll be seeing our Ma next, as easy as paper flapping from that hardly-a-monk's hand. Stop flapping yourself.

The snow's in my face. And you're dragging the rope.

We haven't eaten it?

☠

Not much farther.

Not so far that you can fly.

Seven.

If only we had paper, we could burn paper.

Or make a map.

Or a bird.

Or put death on it, like my paper.

It's the bear.

Aye.

We have been circling it.

Circling sevens. And more.

What's that great bit of cloud over there? Seen, there, in the side of the ice.

Another trick of the eye.

You're just trying to throw me off again, first gabbling over the whale's foul eye, then the story of a fish you can sit on to help you think, then of that detested Frenchman who folded gulls—I swear you are a brother to confound another. Just look and tell me what you see.

A whale.

A fish-whale?

One of these white ones you're supposed to stay away from, a great white whale suspended in the air with string, and snow forcing its gullet like krill in a wave.

It is not. It's a gull too close. There's too much fog to see.

It's a whale.

Then it's come for its eye. Give it up, give it.

Never.

You must.

Gone.

Or just a cloud.

Or we're inside the fish—

—and another's come to swallow us.

Or something's slipped out and gone down below, into a hole in the ice.

By the ghost of all the blubber that rinses these seas! It'll come roaring up next at our feet when we least expect it, it'll come roaring up and rip off our legs and chew us up alive like one of those map serpents.

At least it's not—my female parts.

30

Keep walking. First you see things that aren't there and now this talk of female parts. Seven. I've known you since all the seas were fair game, you bastard, we were boys together with our Ma, our gibbetty Ma.

Seeing that we're going to die, I thought I'd mention my true parts.

The wind has changed, the ice is freezing itself. Did we turn wrong?

It changed, like me.

Now that we're not going to die just yet, you stop that telling of things, I mean we will die but we don't have to do it just now. So whatever it is you're wanting to tell me more of, you needn't be in a hurry to.

You always admired my backside.

That I did. I do, as a brother should on the sea. But you as a woman? You're my brother and that's how brothers get along. Quiet yourself.

Ha! You'll see—you'll be rubbing your bloody stump against me, melting the snow for miles.

That'll keep me walking a league or two more.

I wore curls and a dress until you were out of short pants.

All the young wore them, it was the fashion to dress

and curl. I myself wanted powder.

Ma wished to protect me from her drowning and throttling and the dangerous drubs she plunged herself into. She said women had these ways and I shouldn't be ashamed but that I should hide them all or men would open me up, the men from the sea beside our house, every pirate and captain and huckbutt that sailed or swum up.

I'd die before I'd tell a thing like that on myself. A woman!

Better I tell and we walk a little faster. Seven is the number.

Unless seven is a mistake from the start, another mistake from the start like being from some other parent, our Ma being that way and you being our Ma's way, a woman that is.

I am a woman so every man I killed coming aboard could be killed for Ma and myself, together.

I'm lifting my boots a little higher just to clear my haunch and get back quick to tell the pirates about the woman they remembered smelling way back before. If it be true.

A siphon for when I made water. A siphon—you never saw.

I never looked. I have my delicacy.

I confess to having used your cutlass to cut my own wailer's cord as I birthed him one dark night out of Newfoundland. Out of all the clothes I wore to round me, I bore a wailer from the likes of that slaver dressed as a monk. There, I've said it twice.

The Frenchman who slaved us? Who folded the paper?

Whom I did not trick, I could not. Which is why I believe we were unchained at the storm, why we were not drowned as the others were.

I always wondered.

I never had the rations to bleed until the monk took me on as a pet. Or else the father could have been Phynias.

Phynias with the pig knuckle hands? I only heard about him.

It could've been Phynias. I didn't complain. I gave the wailer over to Molly, the wretch, with her two others.

The wretch we tossed overboard?

She and the babes were tossed, yes.

And you?

My eyes couldn't take the sun, if you remember. I stayed down below for once, buttering the seams for a week.

I did wonder. You hated belowdecks.

No one will take me for who I am, I've been too long at it. Even you don't get the gist of it and you've tried my backside.

It was dark, it was always dark. That's when you do a thing to your brother.

You never were much for exploring.

Pirates are a perfect picture of a person piecemeal, falling apart.

I'm five years younger than you, I'll find the ship.

You're a woman, and women don't live.

There's a handprint in the snow, do you see it? In the drift.

It's our frozen mates' hand, trying to get to the water that's there, just beyond.

We ate them all, remember?

Or one of those South Seas folk—and their boat is near.

Or a new boat?

A bad business, a handprint in the snow. Better a hand.

The first time we get a clue we are somewhere, you quarrel with it. At least we have found water not so frozen. We must follow where it flows, sevens and sevens, to a boat. Put that cutlass down.

I would but I can't get my arm out of the air. Give it a tug, would you? Careful. The right way.

Maybe I should sing. I feel like singing.

You can't sing, if you sing the snow will fall on us, off the mountainside, straight from the ice.

Next time I trip over the treasure, I'm going to stamp on it. It'll have my bootprint then, my own hobnail.

How thick is the ice?

It could be just water, the difference between truth and consequence, or it could be the sky flattened and now broken. I don't know about thick. There's a snow in my brain and ice all about. And a heat fog. The kind a whale leaves after a spout.

It could be ice with teeth and breath.

Or a toothless bird, one of a flock left after the ocean was made.

Or a folded paper.

Quiet.

If you can speak, I can sing:

There was an old man with a single eye
Who danced upon the ice.
He chopped a hole so deep with his peg
He slid up to his arse.

You've scared them.

No.

See where the creatures run up to that hole and look over? See—at the end of my arm. They trot right up to the water like Sunday parsons, with their necks streaked in the colors of the sun. They stand on their heels, the tops of their beaks tucked to their bellies, squinting into the sun and all that white.

It can't be, it can't be.

There's more of them, over there, sliding right over the edge.

Mind the edge. Thin ice—here and here—

Get off me. Your damn leg put a bruise in my shin. Stand up on your own good leg and hold the rope.

Take the cutlass now. I can't balance with it.

You trust me with this sacred weapon? The one you swear by and sleep beside and love truer than your own brother?

Take it.

The birds stand on the edge and then just slide right into the thaw. It looks like true amusement. When we were boys in the colonies—

You never were a boy in the colonies.

Eyes. Just there.

Go at them with my cutlass, brother mine, mine own brother. Take it and fight them that has eyes before you freeze to your death in your breasts and quim. The whales you love so much with all their spouting steam will crack through and we will fall into their caverns—but we will have our cutlass out and thrashing.

The eyes are in the ice.

A brook of chatter even unto the empty wind. Let us fight. We must fight them. Give me that.

Put it down. Don't you see? Your foot is on her head in the ice below.

It's a she who comes at us? I can run through a she as well as a he.

Wait—she holds a child to the crack, mine own child.

Say it is a bird or a seal or a fish.

She is hoisting my child up. It looks like me. It waves.

I will cut this she the way I cut when you and I were drowned and going down. I will kill this monster now, the way I did to save you from the creatures the time we swum.

There she is, as real and clear as the water itself.

You're as wrong as Ma.

She speaks. She says, Aye, and gestures.

This is a cursed game and I won't play it. The sound of this is enough to know you're dead and done. Stop talking to your feet. The ice is too thin here, yes, with animals under it who would tear us to bits in an instant.

Aye? Or mine eye?

I am turning and walking the sevens. First the femaleness, now the raving.

No, no—hold up. Take this eye of mine, the whale's eye. Look through it.

At last, you're giving it.

Fit it in.

It has the look of dice.

Take your hand away from your face and feel your way—

The ice is shaking.

To the shore—you must see her.

No, no—the ice is thinner here.

The lights! See the lights behind her!

I don't see any lights.

I be a woman with two eyes and I see them: a red, the purples of the cloth, a tincture of orange, the color of light.

Take your eye back, I don't want it if that is what you want me to see.

Come, she says come, doesn't she? With all that loud breathing? Let me out of this rope.

I can't swim you know, I can't swim at all.

Just let me—

Mercy! We're cut.

It's the gills of a fish below. A whale. Look close! Stop your leaning!

You've run me through. With my own cutlass, my very own brother.

I did not plunge it, you ran into it.

The blood runs fast, it likes the cold. Not death, not death.

You would not let me go to her.

Aye.

The true brother.

Aye.

You saw her then, didn't you? With the eye? You must tell me.

I saw—

You must tell me.

Mark the spot—

What did you see?

The sea, I saw the sea. And—

And?

You, a she, the sea—

Did you see her?

I saw—sister—I saw—

I will mark the spot, I will. What did you see?

Aye, the sea.

Just one more breath! Oh, brother!

Ma!

Here be his X, one false leg, one true, spread. But where be my sister? My true sister.

Acknowledgements

Thanks very much to Professor Kris Lane, Sondra Olsen, Gay Walley, and Steve Bull who is the best pirate of all.

Some Angels Wear Black

Selected Poems

Eli Coppola

Manic D Press
San Francisco

: of these poems appear in a slightly different form from their original
ication. Changes made by the author have been incorporated into this edition.
ne of these poems previously appeared in *Bullhorn*, *Ajax Anthology*, *Dangerous*
ew, *Deep Style*, *Harvard Women's Law Journal*, *Long Shot*, *Oxygen*, *Poetry Flash*,
Squirm, *W'orcs*, and *Signs of Life: channel-surfing through '90s culture* (Manic D Press).
Some poems in this book were originally published in the following editions:
The Animals We Keep in the City (Zeitgeist Press, 1989); *Invisible Men's Voices* (Blue
Beetle Press, 1992); *As Luck Would Have It* (Zeitgeist Press); *no straight lines between
no two points* (Apathy Press Poets, 1993); and *Any Way* (Monkey Business Books,
1999).

The publisher wishes to thank David West, Michelle Tea, Bruce Isaacson, Lisa Radon,
Nancy Depper, Anneke Swinehart, Glenn Ingersoll, Paul Geffner, Clive Matson,
Katharine Harer, Jon Longhi, Mel C. Thompson, Tommy DiVenti, Bucky Sinister,
the Paradise Lounge, and Cintra Wilson.

Editor: David West   Cover design: Scott Idleman/BLINK
                Printed in the United States of America

Library of Congress Cataloging in Publication Data

Coppola, Eli.
  Some angels wear black : selected poems of Eli Coppola.
    p. cm.
  ISBN 0-916397-71-8 (trade pbk. original)
  1. Love poetry, American. 2. Muscular dystrophy—Patients—Poetry.
I. Title.
  PS3553.O643S66 2005
  811'.6—dc22

                                            2005005474

Contents

I met Eli Coppola my first year in San Francisco, in the dark bars, crowded with poets, that rang with drunk verse in the early '90s. I saw her at the Chameleon, walked into the room with the scrappily-painted red flame mural licking the wall behind the stage where Eli stood, scrawny as the microphone stand she leaned into, husking a poem into the mic with all the real fire and danger the paint behind her only alluded to. If you were a girl it could be hard to command the stage at these boozy open mics. You had to be a fine fucking poet and you had to be just the littlest bit scary. Eli was both.

Her subject was love—hard love, hard-luck love, unlucky love. Love made all the more urgent by the specter of death, who pops up in so many of Eli's pieces you can't really call them cameos. In stellar Scorpionic fashion, the two topics were twined tight as a DNA strand, sex and death linking and twirling throughout her many chapbooks. A lot of people tossed death into poetry, for a bit of insta-angst, but for Eli it was for reals.

It was easy to forget that Eli had a muscular disease. She was always out, always energetically participating. You never thought, she's sitting on that bar stool cause she can't stand for too long; you thought, she's sitting there having a cocktail and channeling her next piece onto a bar napkin. When, after conquering the Sunday-night poetry reading at the Paradise, she joined me for an after-party at the punk dyke dance club MuffDive, I didn't think she was sitting on the sidelines cause her body wouldn't let her dance; I thought she was sitting there cruising girls. As easy as it was to forget that Eli was struggling, chronically, with a disease, it was even easier to forget that it could kill her. Of course this reality was never out of Eli's consciousness, and her poems are thick with the hot, often frustrated attempt to get as much of life—lusty, ill-advised, reckless, sweaty, passionate life—as she could. She wrote about being a cane-wielding, thieving squatter across Europe, against doctor's orders. She railed against the killers of wild freedom, the cops and the rapists and government. She chased down love with a bruised and cranky faith—she went all the way to North Carolina, for christ's sake, for a boy. We missed her back in the city, but she returned, with more poems.

I learned to write from listening to Eli, from toting her chapbooks around in my army bag and reading them on the rumbling 14 Mission, reading them at work when I should have been working, reading them at bars as I prepared to write my own poems into notebooks. She taught me poetry and inspired me to give into my own wildest nature, my own violent claw at love, my own hunt and impatient struggle. She taught me to pet and expose the part of myself most desperate for love, taught me that desperation for love and its most basic expression, sex, is nothing more then a desperation to live, which is holy. Upon completing my own poetry chapbook, a collection of pieces that squirmed and bucked in the loveless clutch of another girlfriend I felt couldn't match my intensity, I typed into the front cover a fragment of my favorite Eli piece, "Suite: The Hot Charade"—

> . . . but I owe my life to these very imperfections,
> my fistful of desires.
> You could call it restraint or you could call it a chokehold.
> You could call it common courtesy or you could call it
> a basketful of lies.
> You could call me the sister of Icarus or the village idiot or
> a woman scorned
> and I wouldn't mind.
> What's a warm blooded animal to do
> among all you
> so cool?

Seriously, I related. The burning wound of my heart felt simultaneously soothed and encouraged to burn brighter. Related and felt empowered in my struggles and that is a primary reason why I turn to poetry, to experience that kind of connection. I hope you not only enjoy Eli's writings but that they inspire you, whoever you are, to stand behind your most outrageous longings and pump up the juice on whatever life you're currently living.

Michelle Tea
San Francisco

from **The Animals We Keep in the City**

flying

You can have
great works of pain
or you can have
great works of art

odd times, poems come: in the middle
on the bus, in the half
awake time, seventh lap
in the pool, looking
up, sometime in early morning
when I notice something about you in a new light
and now
shy and flickering like the smell of a flower
in air I move too quickly through
without seeing
the one, sweet breath

I care for you
powerful, delicate words
because now is a world where care is only possible
    and all we can do
is defy gravity and sense and
climb the sheer face of it all
speaking what we can
even as the air thins
fitting flesh to stone
scanning for appropriate holds
until one accepts
the groping fingers, the grasping hand
the body's weight
and motion

there's always a moment when faith asks more
than physics has promised
a synapse you lean your whole life on

little time for relief when you realize
you have not died

but you still hang on a bluff
side, and the sky is clear
and unforgivingly infinite
all around you.
lizards and beetles and birds
fidget and flurry by
amazingly fit
for this crazy life

and, much as i'd like
I can give you neither boost nor break
if you look you'll see
i'm strung to some other cliff
latitudinally your bride

only this:
to fall
is the closest we may ever come
to flying

Casual Hands, Brutal Stars, Past Things

I remember watching dragonflies,
noting with particular curiosity the casual
merger of things like dragon and fly.
I remember the fever and my mother's hands.
I remember not drinking.
I remember when the word AIDS was always preceded
by a word like
hearing. Or Band.
Back then it could   help you
hear better.
Heal.
I remember the first night I slept   in the open.
So few nights under stars in all these years,
a measure of longing in light years.
I remember when crying was just crying
and you did it when you did it.
I think I remember when beauty
was vast, less   brutal.
Christ, I remember going to the Bronx Zoo
on a train with my brother
on a Saturday in October.

And here's a thing that never happened
that I'll always remember:
Death takes me on a date
I am shy.
Death holds my hand and we walk
the pagan-pressed paths of a carnival
around in circles
for the humor of it
because what other route is there
for mortality to take

the daylight gets doused
with spectacular shadows that gather
into shapes of wild animals and machines
sideswiping gravity

and Death points out
the dragonflies and the stars,
undisturbed among the offspring of Zeus
in the freak show

and he recalls each time past
that I called something love

and he questions me about these things
and he wants to know
and he says
you know
darkness comes and goes

and I hold his hand tighter and crying happens
and it's just crying
and my ribcage rattles
and my throat swells like the bullfrog

and I feel a savage, unsettling peace.

Roses

He was a lot nicer
to me after
I kissed someone he knew
in the cafe. He was a lot
more interested when
he saw me turn my eyes
away, tired of looking
at the back of his head.

I want to believe him—
the quick words
don't go
that make my head
snap back and later my neck hurt.
I believe he begged the roses
in some psychic sacrament to
carry his words on their soft and sloping backs
to me. I wanted to believe
like I did the day
he touched my silver necklace
in the Thai restaurant
and made my body
quiver all over.
I wanted to feel happy
about getting my first dozen red roses
happy that people still SELL roses in satin
ribbons to men who can't speak
the word love on their own.

I wanted this: to believe
happiness and men and soft eyes in the glare off
the freeway. I wanted to lie
in the green pasture in every traffic jam
across the country to love,
despite every sarcastic thing I've ever said.

I held the roses tight
to tease their tiny knives,
let them taste my blood to see
if they bloomed
more hysterically

then,
pushed the vase to the edge of the kitchen table,
putting it automatically in the sun,
ignoring the voice that said flat
out: CUT flowers don't need
sun. The scent was proud for a full week,
    declaring love too late
while I washed counters, poured drinks, ate toast
and tried to ignore the delighted inquiries
of guests about the beautiful flowers.
    Now he'll never step inside
    my shadow and see what my death looks like
    and he can keep the shape of his own death still
    a secret, having bought time
    to change
    things
    dress up
    the death a bit more
    or convince himself that death will become
    a beautiful woman
    who loves him
    and gives him roses
when it's too late.

I can't decide what it is
I keep respecting, no matter
how the irony rings its gory bell on my skull
    the roses? (those guilty gremlins in tuxedos)
    the guy who made me cry
for the love I didn't have
and then the love I did
over my cheese sandwich and coffee at Biff's,
whispering goodbye to me in a poem
about something he'd lost?
It may be respect for love itself,
love that says only
go on,
love that knows
we will continue
to do anything
for love—
anything

anything

Hired Hands

the bad dreams
draw me back
to the table
and the chair,
the pen and the need,
the question and the answer:
    i question the sun
    and it answers
    sun
    i question the poet
    and he gets coy and it becomes sexual
    then he points
    away
    from himself
    i question love
    and it is silent
    i question myself
    and the next self asks who the hell i think i am
    and then it will think
    about answering

the long dead are not that long gone
the long gone are only a hand's width away
    they make me write this
    i don't know who they are
and i write too quickly to capitalize
my i's

what does it mean doctor
when it hurts
at the base of my skull
in the morning
    it means the police are tying a slow noose around the block
    they've turned off the sirens, getting smarter
    while we're inside watching tv
        and too used to flashing lights anyway
to notice

i should have taken more notes when
things made sense, i think
i can't call home much anymore
they worry either way
and besides it's always ten o'clock
once you begin to move
among time zones
and i hope their house
worked for and waited for and waged for
keeps them safe

the muse says it may have a few love
poems left, some resting, a token or two,
a place to feed,
    but don't love too many, it says
    love the hunt
    and later there may be time for loving
    one thing at a time

to fly you must build up speed,
to break through the white fence
is harder than you think
women are still wearing warpaint
and now
pretty things must be laid aside for the beautiful

there may be time for swimming in the creek again
the lights may stop flashing
and melt back up into stars that grant secret wishes

you may stop smoking
when the catastrophes stop
like waking up

trust me, in the dark
your eyes will illuminate
enough

now i stand next to the strongest men i've ever known
and this must mean we've made it to the front:
    ground softening with the inkling of blood
    my skeleton quivering with standing

on two feet for the first time,
soul loaded into the barrel
of the shotgun and the canteen both
my eyes focus on patterns in the camouflage
that give the enemy away

i put two fingers to his neck in the night
to learn him, i close my eyes
and let the quick swells fill me
i examine his hands with the microscope and the moon
and lying alongside the bones of the hands
is the memory of the music
the hands once played, before
hard labor coagulated
around the bones, inflating silver tendons with meaty necessity
and brute longing
you must not grind your teeth
in your sleep, i whisper to him
you will need your teeth, you will need your teeth
for a long time yet
and i kiss him
because it keeps me from saying anything
further

When One of Us Can Name It

The man's worried for me.
I am sarcastic about this.
I am sorry that I am sarcastic about this.

When he writes about me, he writes
about the shadows he sees,
following me, waiting for me.
There is danger there, he says.
  I love you   *You love*
  people I don't love   *I am afraid*
  for you
I consider calling
to discuss with him
the implications
of death appearing to him as a woman
and to me
as a man.

A lot of people think I'm too intimate
with my men.

He calls me
desperate   (on my tombstone
                I hope poetic license
                will allow:
                Hungry)
and I can't help but call him
the next day to say o so far
nothing's been discovered
by complacency. I truly believe
the link between a man
and his shadow is where
all the answers are stored.
And, true, it's dangerous
to hang out on the heels
of those who run

He thinks I have *talent, the calling.*
Our poet-selves, incurably wise-
assed, continue the affair
we have ended, glad to be rid of the weight
of us, our architectural wonders of complication.

They don't have wisdom teeth
pulled at the coming of age.

He knows that I *listen* to him— this peculiar
form of love that poets hunt
endlessly.

Then with receiver back in bed I ask myself
if my caring or my not
caring makes me
strong.

And I do hold the wish out like a halo
over the telephone, as we both return
to work:
that one day, we will hold each other's heads,
when our hands are not
so busy, and find
the air
clear between us.

I dare
say
love
is only wanting
something,
all our lives spent
learning the something's
name, so in the end
we may
ask
for it.

If you want to laugh,
life is a good joke.

I'm a child called
to defend a country
whose anthem I can't recall
unless I speak faster
than speech,
just sing,
without thinking.

part one: holyshit look at that moon

when i was a computer programmer
   i had these keys ever-ready: sort
                                     delete
                                     control
                                     escape
shit.
now I sit up the night writing: poetry
                                                           of desire
                                                           to you

worse yet what i want is
to get in the CAR and drive reallyfast
so as to burn at least one fossil fuel to Point Meltdown
drive to your   block
                       street
                       door
                       elevator
                       hall
                       door
                       room
   to break your sleep open   like an egg
                                           like a Monday morning
                                           slamming up the window shade
                                           demanding itself

but i don't go, as we all know i'm busy
Writing Poems   all senses on call
                               all but the common kind
i tried to shut them up
took a hot tub
steam the dreaming rightout I thought
compete with that toxicity
stun as many square inches of flesh as can be submerged
hunger flared meaner the hotter the water got
the higher I turned the angry jets
pummelling denial back into me
at seriously unrestful angles
yeah and i made so much
CONVERSATION

this evening
and at almost every pause
in my mind
this jewel
turned in the light:
that you were hard when i talked to you on the phone tonight
while steam snaked off my back into night black
   and i wanted you to see that
   and felt bad that i wanted that
      felt bad that i wanted
      felt bad
but not for long oh no
I allow myself any excuse to resume
wanting you
because we all want something that goes deeper
than song
don't we?
     A DESIRE FOR ANYTHING
reassures us
doesn't it?
so i go on pulling you to me   across the bridge
                                    across the galaxy
                                    of-no-we-can'ts

this hunger
better than most
has a name: you
       or the idea of you
       or the memory of a particular smell
            i carry on me
       you
       or the static of freedom making a halo
            inside my head
       you
       or the precise number of days it took
    for you
to touch me.

let me say impossible things to you.
give me the impossible
a decent meal
a bed filled
with the opportunity of sleep

the wild chance
of dreams

leave a message
the tape said
leave a message

the message is:
IT'S MIDNIGHT

part two: the moon in the morning

i call your machine until dawn
narrating the revolution of darkness dissolving
sleep on a couch
wash my face and hands when I get up
as though these were two places where
the residue of time
must be cleared away
in order to keep going   through with it
                                through with it

the last message was:
IT'S A GOOD THING
YOU DON'T WAKE UP
EVERY TIME SOMEONE SCREAMS
YOUR NAME
ISN'T IT

will you mind
being turned into words
on each of the nights
i spend somewhere wanting?
do you recognize this gesture
   as redemption
   as a sincere attempt on my part
      to oil the machine
      to confuse the machine with a suggestion of color
      to circumvent all its maddening geometry
      to glimpse the animal that lives happily
         in the gaps between gears?

because in poetry i can do anything:
   on this page i move with grace
   on this page i can rub my face
   against your scarred chest
   on this page i need never use your name
      or implicate innocent parties
      or make painful, awkward sounds
      trying to converse lightly

        through the look your lover gives me

i will be saying the poems no matter
                           what you   do,
                           no matter
                           what i   do
the poems will have you
with cinnamon toast
on mornings when you are not sure

The More You See, The More You See

Baby doves were born
outside the office window, one morning when I was trying
to define forgiveness. Metaphors
aren't hard to   come by, just hard
to take. .   Come on, it was a Monday
morning. I probably wouldn't have flinched
to see a vulture there, a new brick
wall, a 45 year old schizophrenic undressing
and directing traffic,
in mid-air.
But doves.
A certain kind
of dove: I've never bothered to find out
if it's   morning like a.m. or
      mourning like
grieving.   I don't want to know.
Lately there's a lot   I don't want to know.
Lately I'm guarding ignorance
like it was my bastard and abused child, hunted
by the state, its father,
my inadequacy.   I need to fend off
   the gestures of the certain
wisdom of my dreams,
ludicrous cafe conversations I overhear
by quietly, but audibly
repeating the word   no
to myself all the way through
coffee break.   I need to wash
off the sticky substance of opinions like the flamingo
in the oil slick on the 10 o'clock news. Ah natural disasters:
3 forest fires, 6 sex murders,
2 plane crashes, assorted bombings.
None of them natural disasters.
They call it the news
but it has become one big obituary.
All in 10 minutes. They didn't even bother
with the human
interest

segment
this time.
I found this comforting.

Love thy neighbor as thyself, he said,
this above all.
No wonder we're fucked.
Maybe if he'd spent some time
defining
forgiveness. Or "thyself."

In a millisecond dream, doves and
children in night
clothes rushed my bed,
aiming screams at me like artillery
certain for home. The poems
are for them
    from now
on.

a chat with Eve entitled
Let Us No Longer Be Reasonable

Looks like it was the snake
made man in his image but
he aimed a little low
and hey rumor has it
adam got only
leftovers from the old
tree of knowledge

it was a good trick
really
irony is one of my favorites and sex
too
but
this damnation is lasting
a long time
so many begotten and so many
bewildered

it's getting pretty grim
down here and
i'm getting impatient
for a new man
to be made

of spare ribs
or ruin
or silly putty

or something else entirely

Some Angels Wear Black
(this is a secret I hold between my lungs)

Last night you were with me
in a brilliant machine,
a living purpose of body
parts and unexpected
wild leaves.

Now the grain jars in the pantry
across from me seem naive,
the dust that collects in the fireplace
somehow cruel:

I was surprised to find your head
tucked against my neck in the morning
I'd lost track
of who the child was
that moved
from my face to yours,
and left without saying goodbye
at the breaking of the bed,
as we both lit cigarettes
and moved clumsily among objects
and the nearness
of the body we had touched,
the nearness
of a door.

The grey Sunday was making no demands,
an unusually respectful morning, hushed.
The laundry might as well
stay out on the line
another day
because the night washed it again,
and the whereabouts
of the ashtray
is mystery enough.

This beautiful idea
comes from inside me.

There may be a happiness I can live with.
I listen to the animals I keep near me
in the city
breathing peacefully in the next room.
They would come
if I called.

But even they don't notice
last night lingering like the smell of wet soil
in the doorway,
just this side of becoming
past, a shadow cut loose
that no one sees but me.
This secret I will hold between my lungs
while my breath rises
and falls
in the soft, loose dress
under which
my body changes shape
for a while.

It was midafternoon
by the time I remembered
that I had cried,
for knowing nothing,
into the dark pocket of sexual matters,
the small place
of unquestioning.

I remember now.
I cried.

The Place Marked X

I appreciate the warnings
but yellow lights look a lot
like suns
and some of us   speed up
you know,   for that.

Sure, I'll flinch if you lean your six foot strong and surly
over my startled smallness in the hallway
but my senseless faith
may match your sensible fury
cog for crooked cog,
error for error,
gorgeous chrome lit in the moonlight of its working.

All the reasons you gave
I shouldn't love you I answer:
only the same kind
can do real battle
and to the same kind
the dying is a small thing
next to the love
of heads locked, horns tangled,
skull to skull
in a halo of fire like the ones whole forests
gave their lives to,   gladly,
for the sake of one dispelling of dark.

WE ARE ALL DAMAGED MY LOVE.

It's that simple.
Which face do you
wear in photographs?
Which would you bring as a gift to your mother
as she is dying?

There is a man and there is a meticulous, treacherous
splendid impostor.

Who do you think I saw down
14 shots of tequila
so he couldn't see
me to say goodbye?

All I know is:
me and my damage
leave you this message, the coded instructions
to the place marked X,
where you may unleash
the bold and brilliant
imperfection
that forces each of us to bleed
but only a few
to sing
into the blood

the suicide note

all my life
i've been writing poems
all my life
so people can recognize
something: the loss of oh yeah love,
angst at any age
will do, occasionally how big the smell
of one peach one day
a long time ago
still
is

when i'm not
feeling

sarcastic

of course—

pages of curses and kisses
and revolution and the icons
of a race memory that make us
listen to each other sometimes and believe
we think we know what someone
means by that—

but maybe it's about time
i wrote about something you have to work to imagine
with my own symbols
mocking my own sounds
of life and death
cause maybe today i'm tired enough
not to care
if you understand
or if my pain bears the likeness
of your own
and maybe now i can write
my first poem

my only poem because all of us ache from knowing we always have
only one story to tell no matter how many pages come up white
and begging no matter how many people say that was a really nice
poem because no matter i am still a woman with GREEN eyes and
a muscle disease i wear like the funkiest jewelry from soho for these
are the symbols that you will remember and maybe that i once
loved

for whatever it was ultimately worth: THE STORY ALREADY
BORES PEOPLE BUT IT BORES ME
MORE —

and, tired of being tired, there is of course only one thing to do and
that is to go on

so the web of bones aches from HAULING SACKS OF SHIT
masquerading as muscles through the subway all day recalling that
100 years ago they put children like me out in the woods to die of
"exposure"and that is what you want in the literary world:
"exposure" i can appreciate that—

my breasts ache from hunching around the ridiculous belief that
there is one hand in the hundred thousand that they imagine in
their inner milky dreamy white pouches one hand that will touch
them with Love Uncorrupted by pity or fear or arrogance o i never
knew breasts were so stupid—

and my drink aches all over from counting the number of times i
heard the word love (32) the word lover (13) the word ex-lover (13)
and
the word blasphemy (0)
at the last poetry reading

my brain aches with the strain of keeping all xray vision aimed
outward, always away from my own cellular cannibalism, now there's
an image you can work on for me i could never really flesh it out
you see and for suicides to make the paper a gun is a lot prettier he's
right especially a new one—

but now i am alone and no fury towards government or lover
or parent or the sun or the past
impresses me

and i know all wars to be reduced to this
this spiral down to a circle the size of a nucleus
the size of a nuclear war

no cause is common
because my own cause is busy fucking itself blind drunk
and cold-handed and leaves while i sleep
and AIDS is not the only death spread in beds of love
and i understand
but understanding makes me puke
because it changes nothing
and even a politician changes something
even beauty
even what great people say when they're dead
or when they've given up whichever happens
to come first

the theater is shutting down
i have lied
i am nothing
i told you
i am
poems with sharp edges have clarity
and sharp edges
and everyone believes
only as i would have them believe if only
out of mutual convenience

telling the truth
is always more painful
than pain
and i've never done it before
and i can't do it now
and i wish i could

that is the truth

the truth is my last lover
owes me $200
and he didn't love me
until i got angry and the truth is

i wish there was a body here
other than mine
and tears would come out of the body
everywhere
except the eyes
a body with no ideas
a body with no xlovers or x anything in its eyes
so ideas and ghosts would go out together
for chinese food
a body with no poetry reading tomorrow
to go to
tomorrow
and drive home from
tomorrow
to write this

again:

i don't want to be in love
i don't want to know myself
i don't want to be sick
i don't want to be well

i want to meet someone else who is happy

Message After a Bottle

I'm writing to you
because it's a cool night
    but I'm sweating
I'm writing to you
because a thing is hovering
in my mind
like the truth
or a joke
or both

I'm writing to you
because I know you are waiting for me
at the center of the earth
and you've been on fire there for
a   long   time
I'm writing to you from the deepest
solitude of a motel room
in the exact and calculable center
of Nebraska
and this looks like the door to another dimension
and I'm going in there
and these words are the only hands I have
and I bring only tears
for water
because I trust them,
in their aspiration to be oceans

and I'm going in there
and I wish you'd wish
me luck
or bless me with some of those words we're sometimes
lucky enough to catch
on their flight off the page,
believing in heaven
I'm going in there
with no food but fear
because it's the only thing,
really, that I can cook

and fear is the spice
of everything I bring
to and from my mouth,
like lovers   so mysterious and electrical
and plagued

I'm going in there
because I want
Fear Himself
as my next lover
since every man I've ever known
has buckled before Him

In the room, in the motel, in Nebraska
to prepare:
I
    stay up all night every night
    (faking the hours out until *they* panic)
I
    practice stepping to the side of everything
    so as to fool   even mold
I
    eat everything so in the act
    of eating I always disappear
I
    even learn to eat styrofoam
    so I may live to see the next world
and write to you from there
I will strengthen myself in every way
so that someday I will be capable
of making love   with Fear

I'll ask each person I meet
the one question
that makes them burst and attack, flare up
like the match struck
in the dark hall
and look for my lover
in the tendril of time
while the hall is lit
and try to see
if there are doors

along the hall
or windows
or mirrors
or demons or daisies
or animals better than we are

I will try to describe this to you
but I will only be able to write
as long as the matchlight
as long as I am not killed
and then I'm afraid

you're on your own

Eyes for Eyes

The pen I pick up is red.
All blood metaphors will stand by, please,
as some sullen ache in me tears open,
wrenches free, holds
my nervous system   hostage,
will not be subdued,
told: it's night   lie   still,
carry on.

Today I saw a meteor drop (we know, stars are more
    for wishing and wishing
now is past). Tonight I saw
a big, blazing ball of white   light
falling, once and for you:
an awful cliche, but I suppose
we deserve nothing
better. After all,
Michelangelo's David is being   kissed
in a Macy's ad   these   days.

By dawn I will surely deny this, but now I want to take
a baseball bat to your room,   with you
inside
it, destroying the things you love,
to prove to you that I was not one of   them.
To show us both the difference
in your respect
for things: lamp, paints, photographs,
    love,
a cluttered world.

I will trap my hunger for your pain
and my release here, in an unsuspecting poem,
so I will not forget how much you mean
to me, how rage can beat at the walls of my body
as the drowning beat furiously
against willing water.

Our friends always thought   this combination
of you and I interesting but doomed—   I will stop
correcting them in our favor;   I will start
sewing up my desire with resounding
phrases like: It's All For the Best.
          Oh, Yes, We Were So Different. All for the
best. I   will
stop defending: the special thing,
(the thing common folk   call chemistry,
the thing chemists   call love),
    a pulse, a fire   in the mind   the changes
in time and space
that seemed to occur
with us
together
once.

Instead I will ask you
for the money you owe me, the music you promised,
the yellow jacket—   all the things
I can possibly take back.
And I will rage all   the more
    because   I can't have the baseball bat,
    because   we must be civilized,
    because I can't howl
          even one night
for the loss of you.

I've emptied all drawers and   overturned
furniture   to find a metaphor
to make this all go away, to make it into something
I can write
about instead of feel. When I stop
writing, the night's emptiness grows

suddenly, emptiness meets anger
in the middle of the room—
they discuss me
until dawn
                    without resolution.

By then,
the pen has run out,
the dogs are waking,   far away,
the phoenix in my pocket is whining
to be burned
now now now

(postscript, for women:
it's night   lie   still, no cause
for alarm: I wrote   in bed, the only thing
briefly   on fire   was the cigarette.
                    In fact   I've barely moved
for hours.   And the   disturbingly silent
    disturbingly regular
                    neon   flashed
on — off — on — off —
and on and on.)

Considering That Enormous Place

in the morning
there's usually
light
in the morning
usually
you begin
something
then
when your voice is deeper
when the scars
on your skull
are once again
covered by hair
singing
to myself
this morning
in the deep voice
I look at my belly
in the shower
and can barely stand
considering
that enormous
place
see my own face, whole in each drop of
water and I think
that beauty is something
you earn
in the black hole,
each night,
beauty is a sigh
after great work is done,
whatever
that work
is

Dinner

the kid has a horrendous appetite
she says
next to my table
at the Italian restaurant
in the Mexican neighborhood
in the western city
on a Sunday night
in my life.

what could this mean?

poems sometimes like tuna nets
fetch dinner but extinguish the laughter of dolphins
on the way. i write on the gauzy paper
placemat which is kind enough not to bleed
and honorably free of slogans and
cartoons.

the family next to me has been
discussing the proper directions home
for half an hour.
they want their kid to stop playing
and eat more.

the waiter asks if it's a love letter
i'm writing
and without thinking i say no it's a poem

then he asks if he can put my dinner
on top of it.

My Dog

i kept
saying all i wanted
was to take care
of myself
he told me i looked
terrified
they said it
would all be all right
but it didn't look
like they believed
it either
someone said he
might
hurt me
i said
but it's you
he hurt
the counselor said
take it
slow
and death said
do it
now
i didn't want to tell
my boss i couldn't
come to work because
the plants in my room are
talking and they
are growing
and the room
in the room
isn't growing, in fact,
the room
in the room
is shrinking

my dog says
nothing
and i believe
him

Cross Walk

Man's trying to cross the street.
Man's blind.
Beat and bump at rush hour, rush hour's blind
to get home to get back to get dinner to get on with it.
Man's trying to cross.
What if he doesn't hear
the light change what if the light doesn't see
him what if he can't smell how close the car is
what if the car is two feet
into the crosswalk
what if the car runs the red light runs him down
into red light the car that doesn't see
him what if the curb comes up too fast what if
the crowd confuses him what if they move
the steps put new steps in take the old steps
away
what if he takes one
wrong turn
what if he spaces out for one goddamned second
what if he loses count
of the steps the streets the turns what if
the whole thing's off just
one
ANYTHING
what if it's getting darker and later and further
what if he panics what if he
panics like this all the time and no one
sees and the blackness gets blacker gets
dense as suffocation gets enormous as
terror what if he falls and no one sees
what if he gets hurt and no one sees
what if
no one sees
what if
no one

Before the Haze

I light a cigarette   over my work
and for one clear moment, before the haze
I realize that cigarettes make clarity a commodity
to be fucked with. There is   a reason
for this and a reason I've taken
to wearing leather,   like everyone else:
                the hope
that it will get me through the nineties,
a double hide deflecting the whispers
of AIDS,   random
bombers, the question of purpose, a few
people   I can't forget
and a few I can't afford to meet. Leather, for me,
not a wolf
in sheep's clothing, but   a lamb
trying to go   wolf

I have forgotten   the size of children's
heads, how
unimpressed   baby skins are at birth—
I have forgotten   deliberately.
I try not to forget that   breasts
remind men of thirst, not necessarily
of women

Anyway, who needs
to write poems
when my anatomy book describes
the womb   as the size
of a clenched   fist

In a Time After

We waited a time after
he'd gone, till his ghost had faded some, his smell
had mostly dried up. The corners were still
too dark: the soil from his garden stuck there,
   rich and wet, longer,
so we worked in the middle of the room, the parts
where sunlight had been bleaching stuff
for years— wooden palettes, tools, old cloth, his
place. He'd saved fourteen brooms, which we found, one
at a time, and used. The shed was harder work
than the house. The house was really hers; she'd be yelling
at him in Italian all the time for trailing
dirt around. She had one broom.

I had to sit down; the sun was strong,
stronger than me. The back of the old chair remembered
his back, and I remembered better, sitting there.
He'd sit, like this, halfway in the sun,
   letting it all spread out around him,
the vegetables and the trees and the seedlings under
chalky old windows an inch above the ground.
   Watching things grow. For years
this is what he did. Somewhere
he'd gotten a fig tree, gotten it
to grow in Connecticut. I loved that tree,
   its dark gnome fruits,
thought it was the only one in the world. He said it
was from the old country. I was nearly fourteen
before I knew what he meant.

Unnatural Selection

There was a full moon, an earthquake, violent dreaming,
a day of sudden winter in September in Northern California.
I remembered being born
in New England another day, flung from the hot
damp hammock of my mother into the world
as November at 32 degrees, the temperature of unpredictability,
as I would always remember
time beginning.

Notice how true the word hunger sounds
when you say it in the dark.

There are those who carry too much luggage.
There are boys with the necks of horses
    dancing crazy in the streets.
There are people uncomfortable in their time.
I've come to believe that the sun
will heal something, so I let it reach a thin finger down
between my breasts, draw back the violet of my shirt
    as an offering
of days.

from **Invisible Men's Voices**

Invisible Men's Voices

Across from the women's bathroom
on the sixteenth floor
the astronomers debate astronomy
and baseball, with their door open just an inch or so.
Most of the words they use are completely foreign to me.
I walk the long way
around the corridor
to hear the words
fade in and out.

In my room at night sometimes I hear
the guy upstairs fighting
with the guy next door
and the guy next door
fighting back. They use the same words
over and over. I guess
I am the only one listening.

It was men's voices I heard
in the third grade when I read books of history,
reassuring me that the Questions had been thoroughly
    researched
and the Answers found.

All the graves beside Grandpa's
in the churchyard of St. Rita's
converse in dusk.

The police in my head
and the man in the moon
on a cloudy night.

That man who mugged me
that time.

Between Here and There

you see me but you only touch me at night then
you touch me and i think i hear something but it
sounds so far away it sounds like an echo you look
at me as though looking down a long tunnel even
when you are close enough to kiss me

BUT INSIDE YOU ARE SPINNING
COUNTER OR CLOCKWISE
WHO KNOWS
WITH THE PLANET OR AGAINST IT
WHO KNOWS
HUNGER AND PANIC SPIN
ON THE SHEER SPECTACLE OF IMPLOSION

YOU SEE AN ANT DRAG OFF A SPIDER
TWO HUNDRED TIMES ITS SIZE
YOU SEE THE AIR DANGEROUSLY THICK
WITH ELECTRICITY
YOU SEE THE DESPERATION OF BUILDINGS
THE HYPOCRISY IN ROAD MAPS

YOU HAVE REALIZED YOU CAN
SET THINGS ON FIRE
WITH YOUR MIND

He sees his shadow but not his
reflection.

He sees
his hand
pop out of a sleeve toward
a doorknob.

Elsewhere in the city
there is another hand,
a hand reaching for a gun,
there is another hand reaching
into a pocket for dirty pennies.

A hand reaching for a drink,
turning on the gas,
flipping a switch.

YOU NOTICE YOUR HAND JUST BEFORE
IT MAKES CONTACT WITH THE KNOB

IT WAS YOUR ARM DRIVING ALL THE HANDS
BUT IT WAS NOT YOUR IMPULSE—

let go
they tell me trust god
they tell me they tell me
it was inevitable
they tell me sometimes it takes a few years
and sometimes
it never happens
they tell me i've been lucky
let go they tell me
the fierceness
of your grip
is needed
elsewhere
they tell me over and over
that something has ended
and something else
begun

they tell me loving people
can kill you

Eddy

First thing when they met
at the white high-rise party over cocktails he told her
about the two-headed snake at the zoo
he'd taken the urban camp kids to see.
People underestimate their kids, he said.
It bothers them.

He took her to see the huge faces of chalk
he'd drawn for them on the blacktop,
that hadn't faded
even though it had rained.
Streetlights made the bright wild smudges glow.

They went up on the roof to smoke cigarettes
and he told her
about his parents making him go
to a hypnotist in Far Rockaway New Jersey
to be cured of the love he gave
to the man who's gone.
About the woman he'd married
back there for the child he wanted
who still didn't understand.

About the confession he couldn't make
behind purple curtains in dark booths
back east in winter.
And driving all the way across the country
till the road ended
and Well, here I am he said.
Nice to meet you.

They were silent
a long time,
leaning back on the fire escape.
Beneath the shadow of his adam's apple
the tiny christ
lit itself off an inconsolable star
both silver
and gold.

Or a Thousand Dollars

A San Diego man has been arrested over fifty times
for refusing

to identify himself.
Newspapers'll sell anybody
his name for a quarter.
Describe him too, a black man
who wears his hair in long
dreadlocks
and behaves somewhat
erratically in predominantly
white neighborhoods.

Police arrest him repeatedly.

New legislature proposal
puts you six months in jail
if you refuse to identify yourself
to any city official

properly. Let you off
for a thousand dollars.

Nobody I know has a thousand dollars.
Everybody I know has a name.

There's only these four walls
around me, and I don't often forget
they are somebody else's
four walls.

My name is the only thing keeping me in line
as it is.

What a Significant Amount of Objectivity Can Do

There's no healing
some wounds, you just got to catch
some of the blood
in your hands
and feel it
falling.
In this world run by rabid men
wearing several wristwatches apiece,
the irony is that scar tissue supplies
one with a significant amount of objectivity
when it comes to pain. They didn't figure
on that. Or that
the ivory tower collapsed or otherwise
is worth nothing
to the blacksmith
with his iron
in a boot camp of fire.

Eat the damn apple
before the padlock on paradise begins to spin.
Luxury is leprosy in its last stages.
We can change our names
as many times as we have to, but
there will be no hostages—
I repeat:
there will be no hostages.

The swaying of woman's hips will go on in her sleep
even while dreams of her are scoured out of skulls
by the diligent hands of those who know
there is no penalty whatsoever in this country
for driving someone to suicide.

The father's hand
is aimed at the child's head.
The child's eyes are unblinking.

The ghosts are scared
of us now.

At a Locked Facility Somewhere Inland

Bars make living things pace,
their shadows at dusk
lurch away grotesquely,
but never break away.
The pacing keeps time
on a leash; as long
as their thighs are tense, their feet in motion
the body can be
convinced there is somewhere
to go and some way
to get there.
They're allowed cigarettes
but not allowed matches.
They are told they are sick
and instructed to
repent.
The air itself is encased—
the sun behind a fence overhead—
unruly, unreasonable, held back.
Veterans of these wars never stop
covering their heads, never stop
flinching and ducking against possible skies
falling so it's called
a safety measure but then what if the fence
falls too, with the ridiculous weight
of the color blue
on its back?

He asked me to sit with him in the stark sliver of light left
in the late afternoon in broken wire chairs on the
cement square.
I'm tired, he says.
I am too, I say.
What do you do, I ask.
Nothing, he says
words of awful eloquence:
the knife that lifts flesh off laughing.
they have stapled his psyche together with
clinical phrases, dipped him in oil slick drugs

that stop up all
the holes a body has.

There are too many
people in my head he says.
Mine too, I say.

I don't stay long;
here the echoes
know too much
about silence.

Alternative Education

I've gone from
Here to Here
so many times you'd think
I'd have tossed the idea of direction
by now. But it *appeals*
to the restless, and I haven't stopped moving
for a minute
for as long as I can remember.
As far as I'm concerned,
there are no straight lines
between no two points.
And there is only one
of everything.
I was never good at math
for these very reasons.
I did not do so well either
with history.
I've been busy with the living
these twenty nine years.
I can't speak the language
of the law in this land,
which makes it difficult
to abide. But the language of war
is unmistakably familiar,
though I refuse to put it in my mouth.
And I confess that I only became interested in politics
when I realized I would be one of the next ones
to die. When I realized how many ways
are being manufactured
to kill.
Now they are teaching interdisciplinary
studies in schools. They are teaching ecology women's
studies mass communications critical thinking
and Anthropology of the Body.
These things I will not have time for.
I do wish I'd known more animals.

I will never know
my own face

as well as I know yours,
but my senseless faith matches
your sensible fury,
cog for crooked cog,
error for error,
gorgeous chrome lit in the
moonlight of its working.

Instead of religion I studied the ocean.
It gives back,
regularly,
everything it takes.

Even the moon.

It Was Good

Words made flesh
mouth-made hands,
searching flesh
for words again.

We make love;
and the mornings keep coming
up,

a flawless insistence,

quiet explosions
like poppies.

The swell of sleep
quickens and breaks;
hearts strain visibly
between sound shoulders,
beat against the ribcage.

This blood rush conviction,
this purpose satisfying itself.

From these mouths,
these instruments made rightly of skin and bone,
come sacred sounds
unused by language
(still so shy)

In the Rear View Mirror

It's amazing the things you'll say
to a lover at the thirteenth hour
and mean them, innocent
as a beheaded dandelion.

The pupils in our eyes turn the world
upside down
and then
turn it over to the brain.

Knowledge is pale wax fruit here:
the good stuff is still grown in eden
but there you would be alone
and who could bear
both knowledge and solitude?

Here the answers do not match the questions
and trust is traded only for fresh blood.
Here I can tell you nothing at all
because I can't stop breathing
long enough. Long ago
this whole world
abandoned flowers for fire
and there is nowhere else
for me to go.

from **As Luck Would Have It**

Going Back

I came back here but I have nothing left
  to prove
  no stand to make
  no argument no allegiance no apology

Came back because I'm a dumb animal
  a brief impulse scrambled by love

Came back breathing heavy
  hairline fractures spreading like music
  through my ribcage

Because I knew you here
  because it was here I rested
  here I drank of that cool satisfaction
  and ate of that fiery food

I came back shucking off the future
  for a last gamble with the past
  which changes
  which
  changes

Came back to find our garden dead
  a field of brittle brown sticks
  of the hard won harvest
  only the onions will last
  practically the only thing that made you cry
  never seemed to affect me
  though everything else
  did

To find a few pieces of furniture
  some letters in a box
  deer skull long since bleached of the last of its blood
  ten pound leather dictionary
  the only object we both grabbed for
  beer bottles, newspapers,
    cigarettes in little dunes of ash and stub

I could see the thrashing days
    laid one upon the other
I could see you pace
    while I stood still
I could count equal parts wisdom and folly
    lingering in each particle of air

What I said I pretty much meant
What I am has multiplied and divided
What I stole has been taken away from me and
What I have stumbled upon has pleased me most

I came back
    but it hasn't changed
    how far I have to go

For Helen

Mickey was pretty young
when he died.
But Helen says he'd felt bad since 1933,
since the explosion.
One afternoon, an hour of work
like so many other hours of work.
You pick up your hand; you bring it down.
Mickey worked in a very small, locked room,
alone, mixing gunpowder,
for the Winchester Repeating Arms Gun Factory.
A delicate job.
A job you could only do
right or wrong.

Everybody in that cold cluster of New England towns
worked for Winchester's.
Two men mixed gunpowder.
One day shift, one night.
Helen's father had the same job
until it took his head off.
She had seven brothers and sisters,
and then the two who'd died of flu.
Helen was the oldest child.
She says: We made do; it was difficult.
It's always difficult.
We never had money, but people always helped.
And the boys all went to work
at Winchester's, soon as they were
old enough.
Her brothers,
Donald and Charlie and Jimmy and Harold,
who went by Happy.

Helen was twelve when her father died,
and fifty-three when Mickey did.
He had an explosion too but
he didn't die.
They put a plate in his head,
a shiny metal hatch in his skull.
He drank because
it hurt all the time.
The metal chafing against bone.

To My Child Who Is 52 Days Old

We don't have much time.
This visit
through a prison grille.
There are people watching.
We don't have much time,
but I don't have much
to say.

I wanted to let you know about the abortion;
I'm sure you've heard rumors.
Forgive me.
It is an unceremonious thing that we do
in cases like this, in a world
like this. The alternative is: both birds,
one stone. Some lure us on with a pledge
to the sanctity of life, but how quickly the self same
would swaddle us both with the many strong ropes
of poverty.
So much more effective to break a heart
year after year after year
than just this once.
So you see, in my memory you will be safe.

My belly swells at your insistence,
filling with blood and mixing voices,
we each weeping for what we will never see,
while hand after hand pries into my fault
lines, insinuations of metal, plastic, jelly,
    q-tips, needles, hoses and the eyeballs
not to mention the opinions
of millions of americans
jammed up
in the bottleneck
slung between my hipbones.

There are so many who rule
what they do not care
to understand. And the ugly things keep   coming—

    Watch over me
I will be hard pressed to find my way
out of the vacuum and the glare and the 15 minute sentencing.
It is still unclear
whether it is you or me on trial,
but no one will be set free.
The whole country's busy trying to differentiate us,
to trim our souls
to make for neater law.

As though we courted any courts
at all.
As though we had not worked this out between us
a long time ago.

Child, I will get you the peach you want, if you will sing
me a lullaby, for you are much closer to sleep
than I.

Part Two in the Feminine Surgery Series

I was going to tell you
a story about an animal
chewing off the limb
in the trap.

With the anesthesia, though
it didn't hurt.
After the blood was cleaned away
while I slept.
The doctor was nice.
He made two tiny incisions
that in a few months you won't even see.

My belly is white and soft,
just like before.
In there somewhere
I am told
two secret passageways
are now sealed off.

You're going to have to imagine
the blood-soaked fur, the protruding bone,
or at least a blaze of tough red tissue
across these human hips.
You're going to have to imagine
the fury for freedom
that drove my almighty will.
No clues here to the controversial cut-up of the holy place,
no and no blue US grade A meat tattoo either.

I stayed home from work for two days
though there wasn't any pain
to speak of.
I didn't take the pills.
I just lay there.
Flexing each muscle in turn
while a swarm of the unborn
whispered in my ear
how my bottomless pit

is darker than it ever was,
how absolutely
unfathomable

I've been all along.

Jury Duty

I was told
>to call this number follow the instructions for group code
>amber report to room 303 at the appointed time give my name
>and wait
>for further instructions

I was told
>to empty my bag step through the metal detector put my
>hands up while the cop ran his hands down my
>breast waist   hips

I was told
>to follow the crowd

I was told
>to step back line up take a seat and calm down

I was told
>not to raise my voice

I was told
>it was not my job to question the law
>but only to uphold it

I was asked if I'd ever been convicted of a felony and if so what and
did I do time
>(when they asked the old chinese woman she giggled and
>said she was a christian then they re-phrased the question
>and she giggled and said she was a christian and then they
>gave up asking and she never did
>answer)

I was told not to discuss or repeat anything I would hear or see
in the courtroom
>(the judge repeated that several times for the people who
>couldn't speak english and I figured I could tell what I didn't
>see
>and that would do
>well enough)

I was told to observe the accused
>(he was an old black man his shoes were untied his jacket
>was too small his pants were dirty his face was cut up bad one
>eye blind and he didn't seem to know what was going on
>swinging his head in wide wobbly arcs to see who was talking
>though

        no one was talking
        to him)
I was told to weigh the evidence carefully
        (the cops said he did it and the cashier from the chicken
        place said he did it and the grocer from next door to the
        chicken place said he did it and the judge said he'd been
        arrested six times before and the DA said he was drunk when
        they brought him in and the super at the project said he
        ain't never paid his rent anyway and had about ten kids
        all bad
        too)
I was asked if I could remain impartial
        (which is when the woman in gold lamé from the marina got
        up and said well no She couldn't because
        once She'd had over FIFTY THOUSAND DOLLARS worth of
        jewelry stolen and She was still terribly upset about that
        and no She didn't think She very well could
        be impartial)
I was asked
        to decide
        given the testimony of my peers
        whether or not the dying man was guilty
        of holding up a Kentucky Fried Chicken
        with a jackknife

I was told
        the consequences of his conviction
        were none of my concern

I swore to tell the whole truth
so help me
god

Enlightenment and Muscular Dystrophy

The first miles were easy,
you've heard it before.
I took sixteen years in giant strides,
on impulse, in flight.
Breath-less, care-less
child.
And it was over about that quickly.

I was left with a string of small water planets,
a charmed circle I wear around my throat.
It's taken me these last fourteen years
   to learn that certain things broken
stay broken.
And also to notice the space the breaking has made
that lets the whole world in.

Now wherever I go I always go slowly.
Gravity and I have long conversations through my legs.
I cooperate with the smallest pebble.
I study imperceptible inclines.
I fall and I   get up and I fall and   I get
up   and   I fall and I   get   up
My miles are good long miles.

When I work hard I think better.
But I lose a little more every year,
a few degrees of motor control.
So far always
less than they predict
and always more
than I can surrender.

This year, in a photograph, I did not recognize my hands.
It's a fierce thing, this enlightenment.

It's Not a House, It's a Woman

I can get used
to not having
you here.
I do have blankets.
I've been trying to forgive myself for 27 years now
and the outcome is still anybody's guess.
Forgiving you
will have to wait. Until the moon's
too full of itself
to hold water.

I'll walk the dog every day.
Offer martinis to my nightmares.
Like you did, chuckling.
I'll invent new ways
to make fire, always trying to get
the body temperature right.
I will not take my clothes off
when I sleep.
I will not sleep
when I take my clothes off.
I will wait, patiently, for everything,
eating regularly,
which will probably kill me.

If you're not here.

But I must say,
you'll need more than cabfare
to outdistance my love static
on your radio.
You'll need
gunpowder in your next drink
to blast me out of your bloodstream.
You'll need a hundred thousand tomorrows
just to get through today.

Lotsa coyotes out there
howling for the moon, baby,
but I never yet
heard the moon howl
back.

A Couple

A couple of words.
Otherwise

ordinary words.
He said:

I'm
going.

One body moves across town in a churning sea of bodies
moving across town

No one notices
the irregular constrictions of my throat.

Walking from one room to another can suddenly take
days.

I shower repeatedly
baptism after baptism

in hot sorrow.
With my eyes closed I remember

us kids taking turns being the blind one
on the walks home from

elementary school
and how it felt,

how startling
to once again admit

the enormity of solitude.
To continue I will

have to be deliberate:
find food

move about
quietly quietly

listen for trains,
a cool thief of daily life

provoking no shadows until I dance again
with lust in my hands.

Which doors shall I open and close,
searching the faces of young men everywhere

to discover why they keep
such ferocious secrets

like ulcers burning
beneath their hearts

shedding love
like a contagion of unbearable possibilities.

My home is by the wild river
in the house of sticks.

who am i to say

tonight i cannot find my way
the unexpected rain the muddy ground
the wind is so cold it burns
the trees are wild dancers
held to the earth by their ankles
the path of the rocks is lit only once
by lightning
it is this vision i follow
since then i have surely gone wrong but i do not care
tonight i am the only one who knows me
and i hallucinate—
is that my angry hair in the wet black lash of the branches?
is that your love lying crushed under an avalanche
of unmeant words?
is that a greater storm
approaching?

who am i to say
i go on
i am not a suicide
so i must be one of the fittest
but every beast must pass through the woods in a gale of devils

you, you know what i mean
this strong strong bone song

from no straight lines between no two points

Work Nights

Monday

I was sitting inside the parked car
when the man began slamming the
red bicycle into the car with a
surprising amount of force considering
how scrawny his arms were
and how drunk he was
in the theatrical halo of a streetlight
shining on his slamming.

Tuesday

I turned down the alley and realized the man was following me
and that the alley was about to end abruptly
in cinderblocks and shadows.
My senses swarmed like a twister of razor blades—
As I began to turn on him he slid by
soft as the cheek of a pond
saying quite clearly
Pardon me.

Wednesday

I pulled up to the stoplight
a tangerine LeMans twice the size of my car
pulled real real close,
through my open window came a hot breath
Baby... Mamma... Corazón

Thursday

A man asked me for a cigarette.
The babies, you know, he said, *I work every day, you know,*
he said, and held out his hands to me,
lumps of hissing hot cracked asphalt.
Then in the dark a smile flashed
like a switchblade—

Friday

As I stumbled through the intersection of Columbus & Broadway
trafficking with adam and eve in the garden of bright broken glass,
screaming at him to leave me alone,
clutching the concrete buttresses of Carl's Junior,
suddenly there was a woman's face close to mine
saying real low *Baby, what's wrong?*

and I said goddamnit goddamnit nothing nothing nothing
I'm fine I just gotta get
out of here really I'm fine
and she said, *Sugar*
if you're so fine,
what are you crying
for?

running dream

in my dream i run around the block carrying a fistful of drill bits
at first the area is unfamiliar to me but then I recognize
the hedges and housepaints of 1967
in my dream there are no people
and there is no sound
i run past a douglas fir a dark green mustang
a lawn mower leaning against a shed
in my dream i recognize what i see
but don't know who i am
only that i am running
away
i turn off the tarmac dodge
   a clothesline cut through backyards
to the woods in my dream i am running
up dirtbike trails through the dump
coughing up black clods of autumn earth
pass refrigerators like a row of dumb white soldiers
black tires in ten foot stacks
in my dream i scale a hill of garbage
and scatter a flock of seagulls
i see their squawking but in my dream i do not hear it
in my dream i keep running
through high milkweed
out to the quarry's edge

where the sky takes off from the trees

Count Your Blessings Yeah
But Count These Too

The things that I believed!
Oh, the things that I believed!
Of all the things I staked my life upon
so few were even remotely feasible.
So many stormy romances
with the flimsiest hypothesis!
Such death-defying feats
in the hijinx masquerade!
Such an amazing brain and such
a f-f-fool for love.
Some called me crazy! courageous! naive!
He who called me by name I believed
even when every other word was a lie
blowing it all on the fact of our mating
oaths uttered under the goodnight sky!

Even now I can barely keep my tongue
nor get too near
The charm of his sideways glance
still rocks me

The Doctors Told Me I Should Be Very Careful

We've been holding out our thumbs for a long time. We face the
oncoming car lane, sleet at our backs, ice on our eyelashes. Cars
come every ten, fifteen minutes now, less frequently with night
coming on in between. The next viable junction for hitching is an
impossibly long way off. We had not seriously considered what we
would do if we didn't get a ride out of the countryside in all seven
hours of daylight. We stay facing the dark highway, shifting weight
from weary hip to cramped shoulder, neither of us looking at the
other. Stand that way, stiffening, arms frozen up in the flare of
eighteen wheeler headlights. Rain runs along our tight lips, tickling
and dripping at the turned down corners.

the doctors told me I should be very careful

Outside Vienna, we find a neighborhood construction site on a
mountainside with flowers blooming everywhere, every yard and
windowbox, every island in the streets. We wait till the workmen
leave at night, choose which house for the evening, and claim it
room by room. He pisses a long, laughing arc out one window of
the room we call our terlit, then find one, sheltered but with
lookout for the bedroom, one for eating, and that's luxury. We sleep
with all our stuff in the sleeping bags, between us several sweaters
and foodstuffs, drawings and notebooks, knives and jeans.

(the doctors told me I should be very careful)

We go to a carnival, then sleep on a dock. We are sure there are rats,
that they come out at night to scrounge for food. We imagine we
are hunted, here we sleep fitfully, facing each other with my cane
between us. It drizzles all night, we are disturbed, we have nothing
around us, usually we have a wall on one side, a bench above, a roof
or a corner. Here, just a long stretch of planks, sea stunk up with
oil, gasoline, tar. Before it is light enough for the angry gulls, we get
up, pack up, glad to shake the squirmy night.

~~the doctors told me I should be very careful~~

Older women are often kind to us. They give money and food and directions and rides and once even a feather pillow to sleep on. They smile and nod, no matter what we say, and they are right, it doesn't much matter. Would we tell them we sang Dylan songs on the bank of a river with vagrants from seven countries? Would we tell them we escaped the U-bahn Controller by a split second split a second time? One woman sees us with cheese and bread outside the botanical gardens in Munich and comes back a few minutes later with three tomatoes, three beautiful just-picked tomatoes from behind the locked gates of the garden. She smiles and gives us the tomatoes. They are excellent. We sneak into the garden later to sleep but are run off by ants, attacked for the feasty crusts of our picnic.

the doctors told me I should be very careful

We get a ride at the mouth of the one highway through the old East Germany to Berlin. Barbed wire fences run alongside the road for miles then high cement wall, then cement wall with barbed wire— nary a picket to be seen. Wall and wall and more wall. We are getting the idea. We feel safe while the van is moving, but it chugs the last few miles of road checks, of passport checks, of vehicle checks, of weapon and property checks. We are detained. Voices we cannot understand speak with mounting tension, pointing at us. There is a soldier with a rifle. There are many soldiers with rifles. They fine us for something. We pay. They let us in.

We are blessed with the key to someone's brother's roommate's supposedly vacant apartment. We walk through the city to find it. We walk a long way and we are very hungry. We wander into a deserted pizza place as night falls. We look quickly at each other, one grabs the dusty waxy wheel of cheese in the display case, the other the dusty waxy bottle of red wine beside it. Then try to run with our packs through the streets till our sides are heaving. We climb clumsy and weak-kneed from laughing to the apartment. We eat the cheese and drink the wine, and they are horrible, the cheese and the wine, we get sick off eating that stuff, but we were hungry, and the wine, bad as it is, is wine. Our stomachs hurt so we lie in the beds. We each have a bed here, and the door has a lock, but we forget to lock it. Someone a flight or two below plays the piano, we open the window onto the courtyard and the music comes through with the cold breeze. We are very young.

careful: We pool our money for a hot shower when we hit a storm at the White Cliffs. We stay in for a long time each, watching the dirt spiral down the drain and skin flush pink as the steam rises. Later we go down to the hotel bar where the check-in lady and the truckdriver who dropped us off are both having stout. We are so clean we feel silly, the drinks go straight to our heads.

very very: He gets me a new cane, a slender, elegant, wooden cane in a little shop. He is tall and lean, and wears many layers of clothes. His arm is long enough, he just sticks the cane up his sleeve, smiles at the store owner and leaves.

careful: Nevertheless, I break down on the steps of some majestic church in Italy, give up then and there, on the wide white marble steps. It is so hot tears evaporate. We leave town like a curse has been lifted.

the doctors told me I should do something
but I don't remember what

time
stretches out in all directions
we jump
into the big predatory birds
cage at the zoo
to get feathers.
we are scolded by an angry old man
for stepping on the grass
in front of the castle
a flock of little kids
sweep around us wave high
in the town square

we
are the center
of the circle

poem about driving disguised as
the silver city midnight express

now driving i love
why walk
from one crack in the sidewalk to the next
when i can single-handedly engineer a miraculous technological take-off
take my restless self for a ride
lean on that accelerator move right on up
to the speed limit and a little bit a little bit
beyond

the wheel and the ankle and the eye

got three d maps complete with potholes off-ramps bottlenecks and
    escape hatches
in my head
got radar sonar and a quasar hood ornament and i know more about
parking spaces than anyone
having also got intelligence
and counter intelligence

fire up those mathematical principles
on this late night drive
    heading home from the hub
        out to the rim of silver city
            the blocks moan
                and unfold

the agitated masses thin out
to one hurrying figure
for every quarter mile of warehouse
no cars but my car
the moon is shining on the railroad tracks

i take a tight turn on a wide rutted road
sacrifice the least possible speed
then drop down to nothing
shhhhhhhhhhhh
as i skirt

the underpass
where the cop
holes up

last half mile is a branch of empty freeway that rises
over the city and then dips like a rollercoaster
a big long driveway
to my back door
windows go down
music goes up
this place and time

music loud as i like it
music driving the car

mississippi street

      i've lived here a year and a half now
    make an easy basket
  with the toilet paper roll
every time
  no matter how intensely pre-occupied
  no matter how wasted
  no matter even if asleep
  in it goes

  i know which weeks of the year
    the sun comes in the window onto the bed
      in the morning at just the right time
        so i don't need the alarm
              bliss
      to outwit
    a little bit
  of civilization

there are frogs on the landing
  spiders weaving new webs all the time
  after sirens the dogs in the kennel by the bay howl
    making a goofy, eerie music

  for each of the nineteen months i've traded my work
  for one room on a rocky shelf
  under a war zone
none of the laws of man give me permission but
  i call it mine
    my lair
    my fort
      camouflaged cottage
      cushy foxhole
        it's true i stock it like a fallout shelter
  but i leave all the doors and windows open
even when it's cold

  i left the only dream i ever had to come here
  but at least i got food

books
and a bathtub

    sure homes can be broken
     but sturdy camps built of debris
  are the places i like to play best
the dump and the quarry
the docks crumbling in the winter harbor
the graveyard where i walk
  over the dug and dug again earth
    bursting with boxes and bones
    whispering names
      carved in stone
      to the wind

Suite: The Hot Charade

I. Honest Mama

honest mama
if i hear one more lame excuse one more cockeyed cruelty
one more utterly unnecessary lie
come out of a mouth i have kissed
i tell you i will lose it mama

there you are feeling a little good for a change
spine supple as a snake nipples hotwired hips rocking
kisses call up my animal see
been buried under all this cityshit
been pacing in the ribcage
suddenly seizes time warp in its teeth and
leaps up my throat

one kiss can echo for a long time
ripple through this body
in sporadic, exquisite waves
over the next hours
the next days
the better the kiss
etc.

but hell if the very next time the same two bodies come together
the air between them's choked with defend and disguise
    thwart and withdraw
then stones drop from these kissed mouths mama onto tabletops
lips are sticks and worms wriggling under shielded eyes
tongues thick and dry
words clog like garbage in a gutter

i kissed them mama
it was the best i could do at the time

II. A Rock and a Hard Place

Last week as I sat here by the bar
pressed in by an unusually large throng
I noticed the small place I'd mustered for myself
was eversogracefully being invaded
by one happy dick. I investigated my suspicions—
yes, a roughly cylindrical heat-generating object
embossing itself on my lower back,
and yes, that creepy feeling.

The man was wedged directly behind me
and had I turned to face him my face
would level off at his chest.
Neither a threatening stance nor a good ID was possible.
I said quietly but out loud oh right,
the rock and the hard place.
And you know this time it didn't so much piss me off
as break again my broken heart
For a moment there I felt a lover's ghostfinger
trace my spine.

But this man presses harder, is a stranger, will not face me.
I edge off my seat he follows
tipping his pelvis.
I wasn't giving up
that seat.
I'd waited half an hour for that
goddamn stool
and the club had only grown
more steadily packed
with other men
in the meanwhile.

I pull on the thick leather jacket
and can no longer feel it.
Apparently neither can he;
he leaves.

I tell people this story—
parents wish I'd come home

women friends counsel self-defense
men friends say get a gun
but what I want I say
is a good man.

III. The Hot Charade

So I'm not one of those people who waits.
So I'm not patient.
So I don't trust the holy natural righteous flow of the universe
to bring it on home to me.
So maybe I'm just biologically incapable of sittin' pretty.
Maybe I'm not only counting those chickens but already salivating
for those scrambled eggs
leaving the chickenshits
back in the hen house.
Maybe I just want contact now and aim to get it.
Maybe I don't know a good deal when I see one,
but am prepared to cut you A Fine One, right now, right here.
Maybe you're right, I'm belligerent and aggressive and demanding
but I owe my life to these very imperfections,
my fistful of desires.
You could call it restraint or you could call it a chokehold.
You could call it common courtesy or you could call it
a basketfull of lies.
You could call me the sister of Icarus or the village idiot
   or a woman scorned
and I wouldn't mind.
What's a warm blooded animal to do
among all you
so cool?

Still As We Stand

In what are called the wee hours
I discover enormous crevices
in the substance of my future,
what had been
coherent, graceful, trustworthy.
I've forgotten
the chanting that might bring dawn
to heavy pillows, merciful.

My doubts are pale young men lined up on the ledge, all dressed
in different, impeccable suits of despair
and I must talk them down quick
before they jump
to the death
of reason.

Dear God, there are hundreds of them.

A whole city ornamented with my gargoyles
while I am only a filigree of power lines
taut geometric electricity strung between highrises
hissing in the night
caught between sidewalk and sky
and draining, draining
from lighting too many rooms against loneliness.

Questions, I know, are only air
passing through lips
in whimsical configurations.
Still, as we stand today by the ocean, I ask you
to tell me that everything will be all right
wanting you to point out
the oyster with the pearl
from here.

Neither you nor the sea have much to say
about truth, but then
love is more useful,
is what all the vocabularies, anyway,
dream of.

April Fool's Day

I go to a bar at six o'clock in the morning on the first day
of the fourth month of whatever year this is.
There are a few people in the bar. One behind it.
They are not moving.
I don't speak until six thirty, not wanting to alarm anyone.
Unnecessarily.
I sit here to avoid alarm, to feign ignorance
of the one which will ring shortly and with abandon
in my apartment. I order a whiskey highball.
Just to hear myself say it.
A head with thankfully unstyled but
    possibly infectious hair droops
over a crooked arm immediately to my right
    on the honeyed hardwood.
Highball was enough of an introduction for him.
Snapped right up. Not to anything you'd call
    attention, but he was up.
Drunks, sure they've missed their cue, often overcompensate.
This one launched into a soliloquy along
    the same lines as Hamlet's,
as instinctively as he'd launch anything
    other than more bourbon,
from his stomach, at this hour.
Good morning to you too I say
    excuse me but I feel a need to brace myself.
I yank the glass up and swallow some shimmery fumes.
I pull my cigarettes closer,
    the cellophane pull-tie still trailing,
though the pack is perilously light.
Two more. Then I'll have to come up with two more
Dollars. Or Quit Smoking. Or lose the attitude
    long enough to bum one.
As it is much too early to address these solemn issues,
I light a cigarette. Watch the match spurt.
The flint on my fancy lighter, engraved *ALL MY LOVE*
is shot. My shaking hands do fine with the match.
A short lived thrill, but quite satisfying,
considering the scope of human inadequacy.
I put the thing out a minute later,

twisting off its little burning head.
Goddamn splendid evening, isn't it? I ask the man—or mop
who has slid well into my personal space by now.
He doesn't answer and I don't disturb him.
A fine example of co-dependent behavior.
The bartender has meanwhile been cleaning glasses,
which look pretty much the same
    after he's cleaned them as before.
Of course I admit I'm probably no longer capable of making
the finer distinctions.
Although I'm fairly certain he was mentally
    checking the position of his cock
as he inquired about the failure of my drink to *do the trick.*
So it's nearly 8:00, and with all the bright jagged day
like a bad band tuning up outside, I smile.
The trail of blood I left will have been lapped up by now,
the night animals well-fed,
and they will have stopped looking for me.

April Fool's Day II

I go to a bar at midnight
on the first day of the fourth month in a year of tears.
There are a lot of people in the bar.
They are all moving.
They are all talking.
It's unnecessary for me to talk.
I get a scotch on the rocks
with a hand signal and a flash of my license,
averting my eyes so the bartender will not be alarmed.
He studies me briefly, but I am only a swarm
of shadows shed by bic lighters.
He can't tell my heart stopped beating weeks ago.

There are heads haggling and braying
in every booth upholstered in red plastic,
arms airborne and fists insistent,
rattling the gleaming formica, rattling fixtures, linoleum,
all seventy two kinds of glasses suspended
from the ceiling over my head.
I see nothing but fingernails and teeth.
My drink and I are in silent and seamless complicity.
I don't look at it, even when I bring it to my lips,
but I know where it is at all times.
I pull my cigarettes closer,
wondering when I changed
brands exactly, and knowing it is the memory
of your hands I'm avoiding.
Once again, your hands.
I can't light the cigarette. I'll have to go
without, as I've learned to do.

The bartender only notices I've gone
because I left no change,
no shiny trail
of silver,
in fact,
I left no trail,
            no trail at all.

Dues

i filled out a loan application

and gave it to the post office
who gave it to the college scholarship service
who gave it to the post office
who gave it to me
so i could sign it
after which i
gave it to the post office who
   gave it to the college scholarship service who
gave it to the post office who
   gave it to the financial aid office who
gave it to the post office who gave it to the
   federalstudentaidcommission who
gave it to the post office who gave it to me
cause i had to
sign it again

this time it goes
post office bank post office guarantee agency
   post office bank post office
financial aid office
where it was approved
for half the amount i needed five months after i needed it
in the form of a check representing (apparently)(money)
which used to represent silver in the treasury
   in washington which no longer
exists
which i pick up at the financial aid office
(trying my best to hasten the process)
which i carried to the bank
   (trying my best to hasten the process)
and deposit in the machine which notified many other machines
that i have (apparently)(money) which
   used to represent silver in the treasury
in washington which no longer exists
which i ask the machine
to transfer from my savings account which has nothing in it

to my checking account which has nothing in it
off which i write a check representing (apparently)(money)
   which used to
represent silver in the treasury in washington
   which no longer exists
which i give to the post office to give
   to the accounting office
which is
next
door
to the
financial
aid
office

all so i can sit in a room
filled with POETRY.

that casual miracle

the convertible was spray painted flat black beat up
but running smooth and sly out of the city
wearing "RED ACE" outta state plates
parking lights lit like little jet stars
a handful of hot pink
like a corsage
stuck on the big blue dress of the sky

they leaned back
on the cool cracked leather
and knew

they had more miles than they needed
riding the river of enough
cops couldn't get them for a goddamn thing
they wanted no straight lines
between no two points

just darkness laying down
with the freeway

watching the perky little reflectors
light up

one at a time
one at a time

from Any Way

as yet untitled

i let my hair grow long this time
i let my hair get wild and stay tangled
i let it become dirty coat the tips with lacquer
and twist it when i think

i am leaner too from all this pacing
oiled hipbones faster heartbeat
fingers drumming on the gearshift
mind sparking and writhing like a tesla coil
whose rare beams are sometimes set free
specter tail twitching behind me
like a dexterous periscope
humming to the demands of extrasensory vigilance
sensing your erratic but steady approach
from half a world away

i tremble for you
make fires deep in the cave
sing songs of helix and gattling
travelling at dangerous speeds
i am an openthroated slender red canyon
bare and hard as rock and death
yet blooming beyond my control
i am also it appears
the spilling waters and the awakened senses
the dolphin leaps again in my heart

so come on with you then
look into these eyes
green gas briefly gathered into spheres
flecked with occasional gold

tell me what scientists do with the leftover numbers
the ideas not yet merged with matter
what the philosopher thinks of the barely imagined
the genius of the sky that day
what do the odds trick us into believing
what does alpha do all alone

what the singer will do after the first song ends
is sing and sing again

me i'm nothing
nogood greenhooded monkeynomad
mad gracepowered underwater seacreature
not meant for much in this world
but lets say we eat of the flesh and drink of the spirits
collect the bones and promise to tell their stories
casually set fire to the holy words
then dip our hands in the sea
if we want to we can follow these hands back to our bodies
touch soul with finger
taste fear and not be afraid

the lucky duet:

I. so long Lucky

she calls you
lucky
you never thought of yourself
that way
before
but suddenly you feel
lucky
you wonder why you hadn't
thought of it
that way
before
she smiles at you
not just smiles but is clearly
having a good time
she laughs
and it's in her eyes the laughing
in her neck and shoulders
you can't look away from her
you don't want to
you find yourself laughing
and feeling lucky
she doesn't know you
but she acts like she does
at first it makes you warm all this
looking and laughing
the dark red drink in her hand
she listens as you talk
asks questions which surprise you
you surprise yourself tell her weird
stuff
outrageous lies and awkward truths
and you are feeling just fine
for an hour or so
and then
you get kinda dizzy
kinda confused

you start to worry about what you said
you remember girlfriends & jobs & your friends' opinions
and your inability to get it up
in a condom
and now when she talks

you can't figure out what the fuck she's saying

II. one of the Lucky ones

so
how did that shoe
get over there on that other foot
without me noticing?
feels different for a fact
now it's you laughing
and me stalling
took me a couple of weeks maybe
but i'm feeling a little dizzy
myself
a little feverish
answering questions and questioning answers
you come so close
turn me on
have not flinched
before all my sound and fury
your attention is itself
unsettling

i feel i must warn you
i have been alone
and i have not been idle
fortifying the bulwarks of my private universe
spinning intricate theories of cause and effect
listening to the wind blow
through the holes in my heart

i have lain down in love
and come up crazy
and i will never be as i once was

now i know how easy it is
to misjudge the distance
to mistake
the signs
to misuse
the power
i hear what you are saying
it's what you might mean
that i'm afraid of

stranger

it was night and it was winter and i was
lost
completely lost

it was not simply an unfamiliar road
a wrong turn a missed sign
but a profound and restless darkness
spread out in every direction

me and my car
skidding a skinny tarmac trail through
bled dead fields of cotton, tobacco, soybean, pecan
through kudzu and kudzu and more kudzu
frost makin razors of the starlight

i never been so crazed never felt so broken
reflections of hellfire still flickering in the sockets
of my eyes

i find myself pulling off the road
i find myself parking in a dirt lot
i find myself reading a sign stuck fast in frozen ground
it does not say you are here

it does not say
promised land
it says welcome without the e
it says this place is called the
marsh swamp freewill baptist church of emit north carolina

it seems i have stumbled upon one of god's
more desolate houses
a scrappy little backwoods treehouse temple
and in the dark i stood
just out of the light
just outside the door
staring in at an assembly
of drunks and drug addicts

speaking quietly of the most unlikely
human transformations

mars must have brushed by venus up there
way over my sorry little head
some warped weft loosed in the brocade heavens
some timespace continuum backlash
freeing up my sorry little soul

because there and then
the year of trials began the long process of ending
the season of eros, the season of errors
the reign of terror giving way
suddenly
to the rain of rain

see i'd never considered
just putting the burden
down

i feel dumb
hands clumsy with lightness
i feel
a magnificent relief

i can see
how you could call this
god

well i like the fireflies and the thunder

i was only gone a week but east west west east
for a full minute i can't remember where
the coffee filters are kept
are kept by me
in this shitshack decaying slowly in the swamp
that currently serves as my home
this gesture i have done nearly one thousand times
this reaching
this search for cheap clarity
the southern summer makes me dopey
so i'm lookin for a dose
but now my arm hangs suspended
my eyes wander
my hand pulls back instinctively
to cover my heart

i carry the living around in my body
and can't even call that home
and always the brain in tow
taking up the rear
forever two steps behind
in space and time
remember how here was there
where we just were
this morning
back home from back home

people out here always askin where i'm from
they say you talk funny
and ain't that a mans name
and what have you done to your hair
what can i say
in sign language a flying golden earring
the state of plenty a cornucopia
the ocean known as pacific
though one could only think it peaceful
from somewhere in outer space
a city named for a man who loved animals

a street called mississippi
wasn't born there either
just the last place on my journey
so i know i don't answer
the questions they ask

here they got fireflies and thunder
fiddle music and mountain talk
got plenty of space and lots of green
more jokes and more bugs
okra instead of burritos
junebugs big as alley cats
a hot haze of honeysuckle
stead of that cold ocean breeze
these are a land people
wound in the intricate rootworks of history
sunk in the red red earth
that have little to do with me

in california i could not see
the crown of the redwood
from its massive foot
straining out of the earth for centuries

i can tell you why i left
parting the veils of fog to reveal the faces of the madmen
who lived in the crevices of my neighborhood
feel the growing presence of guns
the dwindling of my dollars
but more than all that there was a restlessness
coming from the core of me
and too many sorrows following me around

but back there i remembered
the depths of kinship i struck with complete strangers
hearing five different languages on the bus
learning the intricate magnificent coastline
procedures to survive earthquakes
how to shift up and down some serious hills
at the tops of which you could see visions
i remembered
how tiny bubbles clung

to the hair on his face as he laughed
underwater in the eel river
hundreds of perfect translucent spheres

tough enough i been here before
and everything was different
but was that really me
and here is a bouquet of fireflies
and before is lost to me forever
if i looked at it that way

sf song

i remember how the girls danced
sometimes you gotta go where
the stars are
sometimes you gotta pay whatever
price is required
sometimes you gotta go watch
some boys dance
sometimes you gotta reckon
with the ugly and unquiet
carry on about the state of things
tighten your fist around the throttle
let the crazy cat out of the bag
turn the timid back toward home
sometimes you realize how fast your life is going by
so maybe you better just get the hell out there
and dance

my most of all pal
(for Lucy)

i call her sweet potato pie loose loosey and my delight
i call her lulubelle and lucifer and luz
i call her the finest little rutabaga in all of palookaville
foxy lady and bubba and the most excellent being of all
i call her lola falana and louie lumbago
lassie rintintin astro max the red baron
i call her a cow and a pig and a werewolf and a chicken
sweetsmelling selfcleaning uberdog
i call her a shithead but only once in a great while

i call her in and back and to me
i tell her to sit and stay and cool it
i tell her to wait and stop and drop it
i tell her load up back off be quiet
and i hate to have to say those things sometimes
lots of times i hate it

i tell her i love her probably ten times a day
and i mean it every time
i whisper come here little missy my little babaloo
and tease her like the witch
with you and your pretty dog too
i say i'm sorry for the way things are
and the things i do
i say the ways of people
are unfathomable to me too

i sing to her
i don't sing to no one but her
in the wild peopleless places
i sing her the songs of my soul

if i cannot

if i cannot write in the calm sunny morning
if i cannot write in the clear dark night
while the dog lays asleep at the fire
if i cannot write with a window and a chair
gasoline and paxil and raid
if i cannot write even though there are no
children no relatives no nasty neighbors (no lovers)
no impending evictions, no warrants for my arrest
no restraining orders, no outstanding debts
if i cannot write under the soft giggling stars
over a cool moonlit bay
beneath the palm fronds next to the jasmine fingering the ivy
if i cannot write with a computer
    that cost more than any of my cars,
a hundred thousand dollar brain, living
in a goddamn priceless sliver of the world

can't write novels or songs or stories worth a shit not scripts
not comic books not copy not manuals
if i cannot write about now how

will i write in prison hiding under
    the house dodging the bullets?
will i write when the power is off?
the provisions dwindling?
when my luck runs out?
if not that how will i write when i'm old?
if i cannot how will i say goodbye

i have written in surrendered and escaped houses
in the 2 x 4 hotel room and on the greyhound bus
in the emergency rooms and toilets and bars and
at the roadside vegetable stands of americas byways
i have written on the seething sea
    and under the saintly redwoods
and in golden meadows with cows
i have written under pressure
    from gargantuan complexes of human nature
under the influence of magnificent hallucinations

written crystal clear words in countries of utter confusion
soaring high above the woes of the whole wide world
i have written of bloody wars in my itty bitty soul
i have written out all
so if i cannot write now what does that mean?

shite! if i do not write no one will be the wiser
a lesser ripple in the literary ocean there could not be than me
if i cannot write, learn to drive a truck
if not write then ride horses walk walk walk with the dog
swim and eat and sleep
if not
write anything
well then
everything else

animals

tender flesh under enhanced hide
thick-zippered snug-necked
not a wolf in sheeps clothing but a lamb
trying to go wolf
baby baby who do you think youre foolin
he croons in her ear
the monkey takes over
it almost always does
she is no longer a lamb no
who eats only grass in its life
known for its submission and delicacy
no its the monkey now smelling
the ripe musks of the living
monkey got the streak of mischief
she's been looking to recover
he imagines a spinetail twitching and peering
at him over her shoulder
as she pushes him up against the truck
his eyeballs stick open as he watches
it sway and snap behind her
hes watching it as she kisses him
a periscope a lightning rod a snake a rope a spring a finger
she's a dangerous lovehungry stubbornminded creature
anyway you look at it
whatever shape she takes
o shit her doe is taking on paws
if he goes on kissing her a few more
members of the animal kingdom might turn up
in fact it seems likely
rumor has it she was a dolphin first so learned early on
the best thing to do with brains is
figure out how to have more fun
been a porcupine too you can tell by the hair
and probably a ferret a platypus a crow
a gila monster a polar bear a scorpionfly who knows
a great many things are possible
in that first flush of mating
but its she who calls it that
(a mating) not him

strolling

when the cute guy goes speeding by on rollerblades
with butt musculature outlined in perfect black lycra detail
something powerful in me rises up and yearns toward him
and is sucked out in a split second
carried off on his tailwind
scattered into the woods
for a long moment i'm altogether green as those trees
for those legs
I want to have a pair of my *own* so I can *blade*
straight out to the ocean from here at a furious pace
till I die of a massive multiple heart attack
and a joy beyond endurance
if body parts were things one could simply remove
from those who would not use them
I would be snatching up new parts right and left
and chasing this guy on a lark
dipping into the vast cauldron of unused brain mass
for my protein drink
but instead I move at the extremely unremarkable rate
of probably one mile in one day
and I think, pissed off
no faster than a two year old
and what do you know if the second I think that
what should appear in the rollerbladers wake
but this little guy
doing goofy two year old trailblazing
a few feet in front of his dad
clumsy as shit, clumsier than me
but loving every minute of his just begun existence
he is grinning a grin to beat *all*
looking back for just a second
just a glance but straight into my eyes
his eyes lit like lamps with wonder
he turns back
he is busy
he is chasing a butterfly
the king of them all the monarch
the big bold butterfly I hadn't noticed in the sky
jerky and dreamy and adept

it is made of *almost nothing*
some artfully arranged dust
in the brilliant colors of itself
linked by something invisible
to a body more fragile than a matchstick
but he is on his way to mexico
this not even littlest of the little guys
he is on his way to mexico
for the mating of a lifetime

till death do they part

Sometimes he comes home.
Sometimes he doesn't.

She comes home
each day
at the same time.
By the same route.
It has become her habit
to slow her pace
and breathe deeply
coming up the alley.
She examines the apartment thoroughly
each time she enters it.
He leaves a visible
and an invisible trail.

She does things,
lots of little things.
Clean, cook, fix.
She is organized, efficient,
patient.
She takes on one task
then another,
then another.
She used to think. Worry.
Call people. Look for him.
Now after work
she works.

She is not tired.
The longer she waits,
the less tired she becomes.
The more nights she waits,
the less food she needs.
She has spent perhaps
forty such nights this year.
It is spring.

She stands at the sink,
head down.

Stainless steel, porcelain.
She looks up.
White walls, white blinds.
She tries not to look
at the clock.
Head down, stainless steel, white walls.
She looks. It is two a.m.
Something in her chest
collapses. Like a boot crushing snow.
Something in her mind
spills over and burns. Like a coffee cup,
absentmindedly overfilled.

She shuts the lights off,
draws the curtains,
lays her self down in the bed.
She hears glasses
glittering in the kitchen.
She smells the pile
of her clothes
on top of a pile of his clothes
from the night before.
The clock at her head by their bed
winks red crystals wink in the black.
She must look.
She must count hours
set the alarm.

Lying still, she becomes rigid
with listening.
Searching out erratic sounds
beyond the bump and shudder
of machinery.
Tracking living things.
Out on the street, in the walls, in the backyard.

SUDDENLY KEYS CLASH against the back door lock.
Memories flash like gunfire.
The plate breaking,
the truck swerving,
the jacket slowly stiffening with blood.

She pretends to be asleep.

The Saga of Q and A

mightn't that be said of this or this of that?
could it be that he was and she didn't?
could it be however unlikely
the he and the she?
the this and the that?

the longer you think the longer you think
that's what you get if you'd get what you got
one baby and some bathwater
your kit and its kaboodle

i'm sure i don't know
but do you mean to say
every time this has happened it has
and it hasn't?

cream of crap soup widely known to cause premature traffic jam
in the eyeballs of those harboring misrepresented
ulterior motives clogging their otherwise arteries

well then was it
all the wanting i was doing
screwing up all the having
i could've had?

question your distraction!
question your affliction!
question pitch you forward shove you back!
fill your nights with high speed dreams and days
with impossible calculation!

when i tripped over the stone the trillionth time
i recognized it
no wonder the going
has been so slow
so the circle reveals itself

yes there
under my boots and beneath my fatigue
the rutted road of my dizzy perseverance

yes there
disguising itself as a straight line

triptych addressing the authorities:

I. One Morning's Metaphor

He shot the black dog.
Five times.
Under my apartment.
Which was under
their apartment.
That's where he shot him,
under my bedroom.
Didn't shoot my dog,
shot the black dog.
Full of holes, red dog.
The policeman
wore midnight blue
and a silver star.
He shot the dog running
up the alley he was
sneaking down.
Five bullets in a body.
So many explosions in such a small body.
The black dog was a good dog.
The policeman was doing his job.
The dog was doing his.
The policeman shot five times,
but the dog did not die.
Fifteen policemen surrounded the house then,
all refusing to shoot the dog.
Who shuddered and bled
for an hour before he died.
Red and black. Red and black.
Fifteen skinheads screamed and wept in the driveway.
The dog's name was Rebel.

II. Her Words Against His

The Girl leaned
(you know
how girls
lean)
back on the truck
liking the sun
inside thinking
about kissing
someone.
Head tilted
back, as though the slight smile
alone
lifted it up
toward the Chicago sky.

The Man pulled up,
called her across
the street:
C'mere what's your name.
None of your business
came back quick and quiet.
(The flavor of kissing is
delicate, evasive,
and she was summoning it
from far away
and so he
annoyed her.)

Well he flipped out like the carney target
   hit with a hundred balls.
Car door slam he across street and she slapped up truckside.
Seems he was
Police Man
(average white male in america times ten
plus fire arms and little
gold shield)
though she didn't say, so he said
WHAT'S YOUR NAME WHAT'S YOUR NAME WHAT'S
YOURFUCKINGNAME

WHO DO YOU THINK YOU ARE
WHERE YOU FROM
(Who do you think you are?
Pretty profound question
for a pig.)
So she gave him a license to be driving, which she was
not
and the name given to her
not the name she liked
and the name of the state where she was born not
the one where she lives
reaching back as far as her years would go
for steady ground

So her name in one hand
her arm turning black and blue in his other
spit spray off
FUCK YOU I CAN DO WHATEVER
I WANT TO DO
TO YOU
lit on her cheeks
like those tiny white
Christmas lights.

She shut off the sound
once he started repeating himself.
But she had some questions
of her own:

Well mister Police Man my crimes are obviously not your crimes.
I can tell you are angry.
Is this because my eyes remain open?
Because my body resembles one which once contained you?
Because when you were a kid someone
    locked you in a closet and hasn't
let you
out yet?
Because I can hunt and you can't gather?
Because you sleep on stones and eat stones and shit stones
and so
who do you think
you are?

III. *o your honor i assure you*

o your honor i assure you
on some of them cold hard mornings
hysteria seemed the only logical response
to this the land of mean streak and measly spirit
i tell you because you are my brother
now you tell me you're so smart
what should i do about
the tantrum of my tiny spirit
the unlikely cosmos coming from the core of me
the onslaught of mumbo jumbo slawfest
that seems to be my only brains
i have no alibi
i am an unbridled bride
you manhandled manchild
i enlisted in the unisex universe to cut my losses
just call me by my name okay pal
but watch out if you do cuz i will answer
no joke thats more than you should hope for sir
it's dumb luck in your case
see i'm a sucker for simple observation
or a half cocked theory
it was drums echoing off brick walls
gettin tangled up in barbed wire
that brought me here to begin with
and now theres something else altogether
shooting up out of the collapse
look i gotta go man
i got a new life in the palm of my hand
and a black truck parked right outside
i'm heading out to the lightouse
where no true love waits
lend me some wild limbs again
what do you say my friend my friend
stranger things have happened
stranger all the time

gold boots

got me some gold boots this sunday
wandered in somewhere aimlessly
but came out with a new stride
can't afford them certainly don't need them
really i don't do this kind of thing
just buy stuff
but something possessed me
an unfamiliar abandon
an antidote to being just sort of fucked all the way round
right at the moment
and hey who knows how many more miles
i got to go
i hope i always need boots
i can see dying with them on i admit it
my awkward, intrepid soldiers
so its only part extravagance, only the color really
the fragile sheen of slippery gilt
adorning black rubber and still stiff leather
i would like to personally thank
whoever it was decided
at old doc martens shoemaking factory
in godknows what hidefilled hardworking township
that there ought to be a gold line of boots
a dirty steely green gold
in boys size 4 no less
or a few pairs at least
maybe only one
maybe these are *THEM*
i had ten pair of black in my day
whose soles i wore right through
to the brutal pavement
hell maybe its time to let my shoes party a bit
the chick with the red rubies reinterpreted
through the tail pipe of the nineties
these are not slippers
these are not dress shoes
these are neither pumps nor casuals nor sports shoes
these things are eating oil slicks

when they kick it will be for real
they make my steps loud and absolute
gold boots good soles
i got me some boots today baby
instead of giving up

(if the camel's back breaks in the desert who will identify the last straw)

no one was surprised but me
the visionary with the big old blind spot

all those long distance phone calls swollen with longing
all those months of careful consideration
and searching conversation
breathing heavy in each other's ears every day
joining forces to beef up that slim chance...
see i was crossing the wild wooly country
to mate again with my bandit boyfriend

that's what you might call the pretty part
the rolling against astronomical odds
but i backed up my heartthrob with everything i had
executing termination checklist:
exit job stage left give up good urban hideout
   kiss a whole city goodbye
amtrack-ups-post-office-packup
all-out-automobile overhaul
going-going-gone liquidation sale
heatlhcareregistrationsmogchecklicensefees
wages & earnings & credit & vouchers & savings & loans

see i feel like i paid
for my three thousand miles
and then he stole his

a heart is thick muscle that pumps without reason and will stop

so i get there
and its this i hear:
just a beer just a beer
just a coupla beers just a few beers
in just a few days a single act can become
an obliterating obsession

bestfriendlover he called me

nazi cop bitch woman mother
bestriendlover i called him
mean mixed up sick motherfucker

i hide my letters and shrink in fear
monitor his temper and disguise my panic
fumble mentally to assemble a rational means of escape
which escape he too was apparently seeking
only by the most opposite means
so i step out of town for a brief
little breather and when i return he is already long gone

coffee grounds like spent dirt sprayed across formica
ribs left rotting in the oven
hundreds of fleas hail my homecoming
jump me hungry for blood
leaping off the warehouse floor

he took the picture of himself at six
aiming six shooters straight at the camera
he left behind the picture of me holding daisies
in front of each breast and laughing
he left the leather jacket i gave him
and took my lucky one
took things and broke things and defiled things
abandoned and abused things
and gone the tiny creature
who used to sleep between us
the man stole the goddamn dog

he flees one past and hurtles toward another
my new life lies in ancient ruins

stolen truck stolen gasoline
stolen off when no one was looking
but leaving behind him a trail like a series of slaps to the face
stole a couple big dreams of mine and a puppy
stole from people who had already gave him
all that they had

the distance between yesterday and today
the difference between lying and not telling the truth

the significance of terror
the appearance of trust
the existence of two personalities within one person
or one person splitting into two when threatened
by another person who loves only one of the two people
when forced to choose
two people become three then four
after that there's no point counting

but
i swear to you
the two people
sometimes acted like *one*

talk to the walls & the ceiling & the void & the horror
scream at god scream at satan scream at the fleas
whisper to the shadows of the dog and the man

save the dog bones save the t-shirt save the guest check
    with some chick's
phone number on it
save something save anything scour everything throw it all away
hey why not
set the whole mess
on fire

tarboro runs parallel to goldsboro
hillsborough becomes edenton
zebulon is on the way to lizard lick
history follows you everywhere

bryan is the builder lucky is the locksmith spooky
    lost an arm to the war
spooky is a drunk bryan is a drunk
a drunk his father before him and a drunk his brother beside
and lucky, well he drinks too
runt is the father of bull who is stepfather to
the boys without sons who are brothers to the man who
calls himself my husband only when it
serves him
whose mother is the piano player who says i am
cursed

now it takes ten times as many phone calls just to keep me alive
it takes the love of twenty people to heal the loss of one
it takes thirty days to sleep through a single night
and it takes each and every one of those three thousand miles
to keep us each from destroying
the other

Unpublished Poems

Editor's note: Some pieces were drawn from an unpublished manuscript entitled *The Name She's Called: Selected Poems* (1998). Other poems were culled from correspondence, miscellaneous manuscripts, and personal friends. If the date of the poem was known, it has been included.

Unpublished Poems

ok so i'm nuts

the traits of the insane
seem to have sprung up organically in me
an alarming irregular breather
can be damnably irascible, unreliably unreasonable
got squirrely limbs, foot twitching and leg jumping
repetitious scratching of an invisible unsatisfied itch on the skull
i twist the bleached, colored, chlorine-demolished
    hairs poking out of it
into little parapets, i am the ringmaster to this circus
of unfinished thoughts

been talking to myself for years
got a city and a dog to cover me with static
but bug my car and i'm doomed in any countrys court
for an extravagantly homicidal ego-maniac
been talking to my same self for a long freakin time
so it gets loud on occasion, it rends the public fabric
draws attention to the scary nature of my ideas
and i don't ever seem to work anything out
to finish saying all the things that through me
seem to gotta get said

imaginary worlds? i got shitloads
worlds inside whorls inside whores
inside figs and fishbowls and ribcages
in the office in the other office in someone elses office
in the grocery store, in my truck, in some bar

i sleep fitfully and dream of a head in a tenants crowded hallway
shot an unbelievable number of times
i dream of flying like i did when i was a kid
gorgeously singular and totally uplifted
i dream of my job being chasing tarantulas
    out of sand dunes with a dachshund on a leash
it is some kind of public service job
i say why can't i use my own dog they say your dog
    isn't trained for this
i say yeah well neither am i what kind of job is this anyway

fucks up the desert, upsets the spiders and makes
the people more jittery if that's even possible

so sure i've lost control, lost total track of myself
like i ever had a fucking self
i could without a doubt identify in a trailer park in a year
yeah i let go caring about some things because i'm just wore out

but you know there's worse things than to be nuts
this dumb resistance of blood and bone
i stepped off into space when the trail gave out
and no one knows why i'm still walking

[1999]

now, and swiftly

what i did officer, sir, now
what do they call cops in ireland?
what i did before i walked out into the sea
was carve my name on that wooden bench over there
with the pop top of a pop can
in early dawn i could barely see
so i did it with my fingers
gouge and touch gouge and touch
i left my name mister, bobby, policeman,
i couldn't write a note explaining things,
what could i explain?
besides it seemed succinct and i wasn't
making good time with the pop top
anyway

so if you could just not tell anybody for a while
is there any way you could do that
because just think, don't you think,
it's unreasonably hard to just disappear these days
fbi/kgb/ira/dotdotdot kind of thing
and if we lived in the arctic a million years ago
i could just shove off on a sliver of glacier
and people would wish me well?
don't let them judge me who frown on suicides
over breakfast with murderers

hell, there's a ton of reasonable doubt here
this carving, it isn't even a girl's name officer
so you had a sleepy vision
slight figure swaying from bench to seawall
but it was hella early and you know you were
knackered, and prone anyway, to thinking you saw
mysterious young ladies during
those endless seaside patrols
especially there
by the little old church where black crows
perch on broken gravestones
and you were really too far away you'll admit that
and there was nothing but the gravel as always

shells and sticks and bits when you came to look
there was no feeling there, nothing special

i mean i know its irregular but i know what i'm asking
and i'm not hurting anyone believe me
who wouldn't be hurt by other things
my brother would get what money i have
and my family would suffer a little less
i'm running from no demons, only tired, sir
and the sea has agreed
to carry me now, and swiftly

so if you could please decide right now
and keep you word forever that'd be good
i cannot go on, do you see? from here, without this promise,
law man, groundskeeper, lifetime soldier
you have a good face and i want to be able to
trust you with this

just tuck my confusing memory away
in your inside jacket pocket
somenight turn me into a story
you eventually get famous for telling in the pub
admitting all the while it could've been just a morning mist
off the blustery irish sea you saw
and that, so many years ago

[1999]

Wedding Poem

Several months ago, my friends asked me to speak in the ceremony of their marriage. Me? I asked, with a gulp. Wouldn't you rather a wife who lives with her husband, or a fertile and healthy mother of two? How about someone with a better dating average than a jillion to one? They say No you do it. I try again. Couldn't I be the best man instead, come on, I know a few dirty jokes and I can toast with the best of them. They say Nope, job's filled. You write poetry right. So write some poetry. Okay okay I say, you've got yourself one incurable romantic...

So welcome to the magic of mortals!
The joining of our dearly beloveds!
These two call and this hundred come
from all over the world the scattered now gather
to meet this way only once.

Shoulder to shoulder we strangers
must surrender now too to love.
Only then
shall the circle be strong
Only then
will stones sing
and animals and spirits draw close.

Look where the lovers have brought us!
Sea and hills and sky each and all
the more beautiful at this place of convergence
than any one would be alone.
See the same in these two,
both the more vibrant as they stand now side by side,
drawing us together to multiply their joy.

But let us not forget how small we are,
how fragile and easily confused.
We ask for blessings today
and in return lay down
these illusions:

Love is no shield against suffering.

A heart which is open
must open to grief.
Love is no camouflage, no means of escape
not reason
not instinct
not dreams.
Love cannot undo what's been done.
No, none of these things is love.

They say true love triumphs
like good over evil
but I think they've got it all wrong.
No victory's needed
when there's no need to fight,
no fight to forgive
no thing to forget.
Love isn't these things too.

(though it laughs beneath the logic and shines
through all my tricks)

Love can make you peaceful.
Feeling peaceful can make you strong.
Feeling strong can make you brave.
Feeling brave can make you do
all kinds of crazy things
and doing all kinds of crazy things
can make life fun.

When you are weary, imagine this place.
When you are angry, remember this place.
When you lose your way, return to this place.

Look out over the edge of the world
and listen to anything that speaks to you.

[1994/1995]

not on the mountain

there i am driving again
another night chasing the tail of that sweet city
whipping around town like its more mine
than most everybodys

parking reparking
picking people up, given em rides
eating and drinking
talking and travelling

then cooling out winding down heading home
there i am driving again

hitting the first stretch
skimming the edge of town
down past those monster machines
gone quiet in the night
away from the city
down to the water
i go
i always seem to go
down to the water

it's usually dead down here
you might pass an eighteen wheeler
a few taxis speeding home to roost
an electric bus slogging off duty
a junker or two

tonight
there's a chalky grey souped up camero
eyeing me at the stoplight
revving and smoking
he's dragging sure enough
like the old days

i remember
picking up the challenge
in the wind off west rock

the route up an absurd rock opera
of curves angles and
everpresent precipice

right hand side sheer down
to the ugly side of the little city
that leaned out off the cold atlantic coast
left hand straight up sheer rock to a dizzyingly black sky

up to the top to the monument to the dead
a single ugly tower erected
on the scrap of mountain left
after the concrete company finished with it
a rocketship shape sunk forever in the unforgiving ground
this in the memory of the many
of the soldiers and sailors assailed
the untold unanswerable dead
the horrifically dead
the slaughtered youth
the virgin sacrifice
all over again

imagine even a slight wind bearing
the death smell of that much blood

but the monument was of no consequence
to us
it was a hunk of concrete
could conceal cops
a pinnacle of graffiti
messages from generations before us
but behind us
blind to us
as we were blind
as we are blind

and here's crazy camero
daring me
daring
has to be a kid
probably high
look at us

we're sitting at this strungout lonesome stoplight
out on the edge i suppose but not
much of an edge
not on the mountain not on the cliff
me at least moved on from that particular cusp
christ his car is snorting sex at my beat up little honda

so what the hell it's wednesday
i don't have anything to do
i take him on
sure i got something to show him
but who bets
it won't be what he's looking for

me i know this street
timing of the lights
lane changes
the hidden overpass
the violent interruptions
in gravity
he's paying too much attention to me
to notice
amidst the genuine panic in his heart

i don't beat him per se
but i got it all over him
got switch and glide
shift heel swivel head
i got a better touch
untroubled senses
i got synchronicity
yeah and i got years on that boy
all lurch and lapse and lunge
chug and choke
we go a good three quarter mile
then i drop back suddenly
laughing
i see his face turned back toward me
as his destination speeds on ahead
without him
his face stays in my mind awhile
confused, deflated
but somehow tender

bitch to bitch

honkybitchcunt!
dyke! ugly!
bitch!

he blocked the alley easily
with his mangled maroon luxury automobile
swung his beer gut out
and stood on the street
like a huge toad
a livid stupidity

might've been funny if it wasn't
he could kill me
so easily so easily

he had on big black sunglasses
but i recognized the look in his eyes
my hatred rose to meet it
as he advanced
a column of fire
a torch in my chest
words shot out of his mouth like puke
my jaw twisting and grinding
to keep my mouth shut

over his shoulder i see

his woman
in the passenger seat
staring at some point
far off in the distance
arm trailing
out the open window

hostage

intricate nuances of my personal identification
are the property of BILLIONS of machines
the vips of the irs and the fbi and the hmo and the triple a
they got my hiv and my trw and my gpa and my eta
and my ovaries
are on the agenda too
in the usa
land of the free
and home of the slave

when they come for the formula of my precise chemical scent
i'm definitely
outa here
i think it's a good idea to decide exactly
   where you'd draw that line
so you will recognize the sanctity of the moment
when you step over it

i have seen too many good young shoulders
   foldandfall like napkins to the floor

so i approached the bench
with my heart in my fist
and slopped that red fleshy mass
down as exhibits A through Z
and so on

to charge this country
for taking my firstborn
as a tax this year

but i could not speak
the language
of great machines

now all i want is to be
beautiful
i want my body
to be the perfect athlete

of pain
i want the wind
to decide my features
and everything i've ever seen
to remain in my eyes

the birth of a flying thing

in love i have emerged
from an egg split long ago but alas
still in a coma
of disbelief
hatching may not look like much
from the outside
but believe me
the escape was terrifying
bone dome of what i thought was my skull
shattered
and in a split second the world
expanded exponentially
quite more than i'd imagined
i emerged
blinking and stiff and bad-tempered
go stretch to find
wings!
tucked in where my shoulders had been
webs of bone
trembling with premonition
crown and shelter my body
sack of fleshy thumpings and blood mutterings
i think no no now
alone these bonds are not much
noble seeming suggestions
blueprints for a miracle
but as i lift
a leathery skin
draws taut between the prongs of the wing's fan
sheaf of skin joining the bones with yearning
as the wing reaches its span the torso is
lifted a few inches from the ground
with ease and an inhuman strength
drawn directly from the human in the heart
as the wing reaches its span the torso
   is lifted a few inches from the ground
with ease and an inhuman strength drawn
   directly from the human in the heart

frankie and the flower girl

hey look frankie
   that girl with the bucket of flowers
   leaning against the cigarette machine
   with the windbreaker on
   christ shes young
   just a kid really
well i don't know what about her
just look at her wouldja
   i think i seen her down on army street this afternoon
   trying to sell them half-dead plastic-wrapped carnations
   to cars coming off the freeway from south city
   looks like she hasn't sold one even
   hell a dollar a flower is a long road to rent
   what a life huh
no really i'm sure
i tell you i seen her before
or someone like her maybe
   but i never seen one of them sell one of those things
   they don't speak english those girls
   just flower sir flower maam
   one dollar only a dollar
   seen em in cafes and restaurants
   slipping through those punk clubs and
    jazz joints and the baddest old bars
   two or three in the morning they hit the allnight taquerias
   and end up selling flowers for
    gods sake outside the liquor stores
   at fucking dawn
well yeah so what if i do what about it
i bet that girl covers more miles in one night
than you cover in a month
and complains a lot less
you shithead
there look at her
   just look at her
   there in the doorway with the light on her like that
   shes going back out into the rain
aw fuck you frankie
you wish you ever looked so good in your whole life

as she looks miserable
yeah i do know her
now that you mention it yeah frankie
whats it fuckin to ya

the line between ignorance and innocence is not a line

skinny kids play armies
outside the First Holy Church of God
on the sidewalk
scrambling holy terrors
chasing each other
good shoes' heels rasping
around corners
stifling giggles and shouts
and sound effects
so as not to get caught

a storefront away
mass is in progress

framed by thin yellow curtains
the overlit windows
stick out in a neighborhood of dark bars
and subdivided miseries
while thirty sober-clothed backs
kneel or stand or sway
none of them sitting in the folding chair rows
women clutch kerchiefs
white lace on their bobbing heads
men raise their arms
in suits that aren't made
for hailing the almighty

they occasionally
cry out
shake
collapse

they wail they bellow they sing

outside sirens rise and fall
junkies whisper
voters grumble
gangs seethe
old men rub their eyes
kids huddle in a doorway
planning their siege of the city night

A Bargain

No need to fear me.
I am too busy surviving
to do any harm.
The way I see it,
if it wasn't bum limbs
or lolling tongues,
it'd be a blind eye
or a firestorm.
It'd be an overzealous forceps
or an unending betrayal.
Hell, it'd be three days in the Newark airport at New Year's
with big ideas and no money.
If it wasn't MS or MD,
it'd be OD or IV,
if it wasn't these tears
it'd be other tears.
These are not answers I gather, sister,
but riddles and music,
and the touch of my lips to your cheek.
Until we are dead,
we are
not.

what i might do with a boyfriend if i had one

first take off
one fine spring day
then take that boyfriend out sailing
and try to scare the shit out of him

that sounds mean
but it isn't
everyone ought to get out there
and have a good thrash
with the elements

i'd watch him
watch him and wind
him and waves and him
in boat i am bucking like bronco

check if he
adjusts or resists
read his body
for revelations
pride and power and instinct

i would speak only briefly
and then only in riddles
he couldn't hear
above the sea
anyway

then slip into the peaceful sunny straits
run her wing on wing
long and slow and steady

maybe he lies himself down in the sun and closes his eyes

after we dry out by a fire
drink irish coffees from a thermos
maybe he says
that was a fine ride and i say

it's not over yet
and drive us down the coast
aflame with twilight

maybe we stop at the boardwalk
and take on some rollercoasters
play us some pool
sneak in a motel pool and go swimming

maybe we drive back up the same freeway
but it is dark
and nothing is the same

follow a trail
of broken white lines
along the ground
the vast black night shimmering
all around us

maybe i'd ask him what he'd seen
and where been
listening to his voice disembodied
as i drove

the bone dry hills
above the deep blue sea
slowly take shape
before us
blushing again with color

we could find ourselves a truckstop
and eat breakfast
drink thick coffee out of thick cups
maybe there'd be one of those table jukeboxes
and we'd discover we like
the same songs

laughing each at each other's surprise

well just a quick one

going to cry it dry
with no stopping till its done
bone ache turned to dust
while all the water in all the
world is spending from my eyes
downturned from what heaven is the sky
before i die before i die
yeah i want to cry like that just
once before i die

not accident not poverty not pain
not even the vast unknown
it's only people make me
want to kill my own
death itself does not sadden me as people do
they make me want to die
sometimes we do

stuck like cement in our proved-wrong ways
what else might we have done with all those days
if all you see is enemies that's all there'll be
immediately or eventually

gotta once more gallop
down the beach this time on my own
heart high with horsespeed
till i swear we're gonna fly
before i die, before i die
yeah i want to ride like that
just once before i die

we're so busy checking back we never look around!
so hotair filled we forget about the ground!
and you know how that one goes
around and around and around
i want to meet someone willing to stand still
someone to pant with up the motherfucking hill
is that too much to ask for if that's what i'm throwing in
a clean hard game i can win

sparks catching fire in these words now
i ain't got much time
gotta say good-bye somehow
before i die

[2000]

make of me many miracles

don't care anymore, don't want to
about any of it, this life
cared plenty already, already more than my share
am no longer interested, in any of it, this life
people die all the time, every fucking nanosecond
and the world goes on just dandy
is relieved to shake them off
it will go on and on till the whole thing blows
i'm just blowing early that's all
i pass on this dumb smudge of space to another
maybe make room for a couple more
rocks or flowers or laughs
i want to go now
leave a marginally useful body
instead of completely depleting it
over another consumptive span
give the pieces of me
to those who need them so badly
and want to live so much
make of me many miracles
a great deal for a wornout woman
a last shot at something like salvation
take the burden of me away from my dearest
let them conserve themselves for their own hard lives
and the beautiful beautiful children
make me seeds of memory instead
safe to grow in their sacred hearts
it is so important that everyone understand
i do this for me, i just want to go now
i seek an open space, i seek to leave my body
go see if there's another world i belong in
a form somewhere out there in need of a spirit
especially if it's like sleep, even if it's nothing
i have lived as well as i could
so i fear nobody's gods
wrath and cruelty have already crippled me
here among my kin
i regret nothing and know that i'm loved
welcome the closing eyes of this too-full consciousness

have used up all my strength, don't want anymore
let me fall just let me fall
don't want the world all newly infused with meaning
another pretty dress of handspun illusion
that won't hold up beyond a few good parties
rather shed than hide this flesh now
let the poking-out bones emerge
i want desire to end
and pity and pretense and poetry
making the best of it is a Sisyphusian to the end kind of thing
i see that now and frankly i'm not up to it
i can't even live without kisses

[1999]

About the Author

JoAnn Elizabeth (Eli) Coppola was born November 11, 1961, and grew up in Hamden, Connecticut. She was diagnosed with Muscular Dystrophy in her early 20s. After graduating from Connecticut College, Eli moved to San Francisco in 1985 and became involved in the local spoken word/poetry scene. Five chapbooks of her poetry were published: *The Animals We Keep in the City* (Zeitgeist Press, 1989); *Invisible Men's Voices* (Blue Beetle Press, 1992); *As Luck Would Have It* (Zeitgeist Press); *no straight lines between no two points* (Apathy Press Poets, 1993); and *Any Way* (Monkey Business Books, 1999). Eli died of a heart attack in 2000, at the age of 38.

In the late '80s and early '90s, Eli worked at the UC Berkeley Women's Studies Program; for a while, she was June Jordan's assistant. Eli completed an MFA at SF State in 1994, then moved to North Carolina, returning to SF in 1996. From 1998 until her death, she managed the SF State Poetry Center. As a performer, Eli read at many venues, including women's conferences, and shelters for battered women and at-risk youth. Eli traveled widely — usually on her own — was a crackerjack sailboat skipper, a good cook, rode horses, and gardened when backyards permitted. She loved theater and music, and continued to do readings of her work right up to the end.

In the late '90s, Eli's illness began to make all this activity increasingly difficult. What MD takes it does not give back. In 1999, the disease seemed to be accelerating, and that winter she wrote some of her bleakest poems. Yet in 2000, she found new strength and started writing again after a dry spell. The crisis, for the time being, seemed to be over. A week before she died, Eli went to the ER for what was seemingly a minor heart attack. The tests were inconclusive. A week later, she was supposed to meet a friend at a play but never arrived. Worried, her friend dropped by after the show, and had friends who lived upstairs open her apartment. Eli had died between 6 and 10 p.m., April 2, 2000, all dressed up for a night on the town. The fact that she was well dressed for death would probably have appealed to her.

The editor is grateful that Eli's work will once again find a readership, and would like to thank her many devoted friends — Stephen Pelton, Silke Vom Bauer, Skye Alexander, Jandy Nelson, and Mark Routhier, as well as many others — who provided assistance, advice and great enthusiasm for this book. Thanks also to Eli's parents, Joe & Ann Coppola.

Most of all, though, I would like to thank Eli, who wrote so well in the face of such obstacles.

David West, editor